CINDERELLA'S
NEW YORK FLING

CINDERELLA'S NEW YORK FLING

CARA COLTER

MILLS & BOON

First published in Great Britain 2020
by Mills & Boon, an imprint of HarperCollins*Publishers*
1 London Bridge Street, London, SE1 9GF

Large Print edition 2020

© 2020 Cara Colter

ISBN: 978-0-263-08518-1

MIX
Paper from
responsible sources
FSC
www.fsc.org
FSC™ C007454

This book is produced from independently certified
FSC™ paper to ensure responsible forest management. For
more information visit www.harpercollins.co.uk/green.

Printed and bound in Great Britain
by CPI Group (UK) Ltd, Croydon, CR0 4YY

To Ally Blake and Sophie Pembroke.
There was a knock on my door one day,
and two lovely strangers stood there
and said, *'Can you come out and play?'*

PROLOGUE

IT ALL HAPPENED so quickly.

But then, that is probably what most people would say of a catastrophe. One hardly gets out of bed in the morning meticulously planning for disaster. No, it has a tendency to spring on one when it is least expected. At my advanced age—seventy-four—things going awry should hardly take me by surprise.

But they do, and it did.

I was walking through Faelledparken, delighted with both my escape from my tiresome head of security and with how the famous Copenhagen park had been transformed for the Annual Ascot Music Festival, held in a different country every summer.

The park had been turned into a lovely little village of colorful tents that featured all kinds of drinks, food, trinkets and souvenirs. There were smaller stages scattered throughout for some of the less well-known singers and bands to perform. Street performers juggled and did cart-wheels and magic tricks.

This year's festival was titled *Carlene to Celine and Everything in Between.* I thought it was very catchy and modern, though one of the PR men—they prefer the term "marketing executive" now—had the audacity to roll his eyes when I suggested it. I wished, for a very brief moment, that the super suave, *I'm the expert on everything* man, with his hyphenated name, was walking with me to see how that title was displayed everywhere, eclipsed by the much larger *Ascot Presents.*

The name Ascot even eclipsed Carlene, which, of course, was my intention, though I would act properly horrified if anyone pointed it out as the shameless publicity move for Ascot that it was. When I took my inherited family fortune to the next level—the Ascot brand was now a household name in products that ranged from pharmaceuticals to kitchen faucets—I learned that women in business had to be shrewd and smart, and very careful not to let anyone know just how shrewd and how smart they were.

Carlene herself, the headline act, would be performing in about fifteen minutes and throngs of people were heading through the park to the stadium. Certainly no one took any notice at all of me, a gracious elderly lady in a colorful head scarf, sunglasses and a sweater that was...er... perhaps a touch bulky.

It was all very exciting, and there was a kind of energy to the crowd that was invigorating. But little by little I began to feel that familiar bombardment that reminded me why I avoided crowds.

That man needs some vitamin C.

That woman needs a baby.

The thoughts were coming faster and faster and were followed by a heightened perception of the crowds being quite crushing and the evening being very warm.

I hadn't exactly counted on the heat when I thought of Denmark on a summer's evening or when I stuffed Max under my sweater.

People are always so quick to offer their judgments, and I'm sure many people would say having a dachshund snuggled under my sweater at such a crowded venue was practically inviting trouble.

But Max suffers from separation anxiety and it had been made worse by jet lag and a hotel room he was unfamiliar with. The poor little fellow could hardly go pee he was so discombobulated. The only place he seemed to settle was under my sweater. I felt a bit like a mother kangaroo with her joey, a nice feeling, since I had never had children myself.

That nice feeling lasted precisely until I walked by a performer who chose the very moment of my passing to clank a pair of oversize cymbals together.

Max let out a yelp, scrambled up my belly and chest leaving, I'm sure, a trail of red welts that marked his desperation.

He exploded out the neckline of my sweater, leaped onto my shoulder and hesitated for only one brief moment before he launched himself over my back.

I whirled in time to see him hit the ground and tumble. He was wearing the most adorable little sailor outfit and the hat fell off. He found his feet and raced off, in the opposite direction of the crowds heading to the stadium.

"Max!"

You would think the desperation in my voice would have been enough to stop the little bugger, but no, he cast one glance back at me, looking distinctively pleased, not frightened in the least, and quickly lost himself in the sea of legs marching toward me.

I practically risked my life to rescue the hat from the crush of stamping feet before attempting to follow him. I can't describe the pure panic I was feeling, clutching his jaunty little hat to my chest. That little dog is my whole world. I practically own the earth, and in that second, I was aware I would trade every single bit of my fortune for him.

The futility of trying to follow him soon became apparent. I could not make my way through the crowds. Frankly, it was like being in a nightmare where you are trying to run and you cannot move.

My invisibility was terrifying. It was as if no one saw me at all as I pushed the wrong way. I got only brief, annoyed glances, as if I had been drinking too much. As if to confirm the worst suspicions of all these strangers, I suddenly stumbled and felt my ankle turn. Pain shot through it.

I allow myself very few vulnerable moments, but there I stood, paralyzed and trembling, wondering if my ankle, which felt as if a red-hot poker had been thrust through it, was going to give out on me. If it did, surely I would be trampled.

And then she appeared, like an angel. A young woman stopped in that endless push toward the Carlene concert, and looked at me. People flowed around us unceasingly, as if we were two rocks in a stream.

I knew right away she was a good person. Her eyes were huge and brown and probably the gentlest eyes I had ever seen.

"Are you all right?" she asked me. She spoke English, without an accent, which made me think she was North American. She touched my shoulder.

I practically threw myself into her arms and instead of pushing me away, as if she was being accosted by a crazy person, her arms folded around me.

She was very slender, and yet she felt ten feet tall and enormously strong.

"My dog," I sobbed. "He's escaped. He went that way."

Feeling foolish and old I stepped back from her embrace, wincing at the pain in my ankle, and pointed a quavering arm in the direction Max had gone.

It was then I noticed she was with a man. He was one of those supremely attractive types, who have an inborn knowledge of their own superiority. He had that way about him, of a very good-looking man, as if he was doing this woman some kind of favor by being with her. Even though she was being protective of me, I actually, despite my distress, felt very protective of her.

"Ralph," she said, pronouncing it in the German way, *Rolf,* "this poor woman has lost her dog. Can you go find him?"

He gave her an astonished glare and looked, rather pointedly, at his very expensive wristwatch. It was clear he didn't want to miss the opening song of the concert, had probably put out a lot of money for front row seats.

The woman gave him a look.

I saw right away that she was seeing things about him that she had not seen before or maybe had seen but, in the heat of romance, had dismissed. I think he saw her blossoming awareness, too, because he turned begrudgingly to me and with the outmost reluctance asked after the dog.

"What kind of dog?"

"He's a dachshund. He's wearing a sailor suit."

The man—I decided I hated him in general, and him for her in particular—raised an eyebrow at her that spoke absolute volumes. *We're going to miss Carlene's opening set for a crazy old lady who probably doesn't even own a dog.* But he set off the way they had come.

"His name is Max," I called out helpfully, but I realized that man was not going to go through the crowd shouting for the dog.

I began to tremble uncontrollably, partly from the pain in my ankle, but mostly from thinking of Max lost out there in this absolute sea of people.

"Are you hurt?" the young woman asked me.

"I seem to have turned my ankle."

She quickly had her shoulder under my arm, and again I realized she was much stronger than she appeared. She practically carried me out of the press of the crowd and off to a tea stand set up under a colorful yellow-striped awning, with a scattering of mismatched plastic tables and chairs under it.

A young woman was just getting up from a table. She was clutching her Carlene ticket as if she had waited her whole life for this moment. She saw me, crying, and she saw my angel, and she hesitated, and then made a decision.

"Is everything all right?" she asked, approaching us. She had short dark hair and she was quite petite, like she could be cast for Tinker Bell in *Peter Pan*. She had some kind of instrument slung over her shoulder in a case—perhaps a violin or a ukulele, making me think that, as well as being desperate to see the Carlene concert, she might be one of the lesser known performers here. She was British, like me, and for some reason I found that quite comforting.

"Not really. My friend has lost her dog. And hurt her ankle, I'm afraid."

Friend.

Not *Crazy lady keeping her from the concert.*

"Oh, dear," she said, and then I had *two* angels, as she rushed to support my other side. The tent café was empty—of course it was, everyone was heading to the concert—so we had no problem finding a nearby table.

"Do you think you need medical attention?" the British girl asked.

"I need my dog!" I said and my voice came out in an embarrassingly quavering wail.

"What kind of dog?" she asked gently.

Again, I was so grateful not be asked why I had brought a dog to the event. Even though Denmark is one of the most dog-friendly nations I have ever visited, obviously bringing Max this evening had been pushing it just a wee bit.

"A dachshund."

She won me forever when she smiled at me, her green eyes sparking with good humor, and said, "I adore dachshunds. What's his name? I'll go have a look."

"His name is Max." I hesitated a moment, thinking of the man's reaction, but anything that would help had to be divulged. "He's wearing a sailor suit."

"A dachshund in a sailor suit," she said. "Honestly, you have made my day. Maybe my whole week."

This from someone on her way to the most coveted concert of the year! But she put the Carlene ticket in her pocket, as if it didn't matter a whit to her, and was soon lost in that crowd, shouting after Max.

My remaining angel went and fetched me a cup of hot tea.

She was just the loveliest girl in an understated kind of way. She was dressed in a rather unexciting pair of capris and a knit tank top I could only describe as the color of porridge. Aside from her eyes, which were quite astonishing in both the doe-darkness of them and their size, she was what I might call plain. She had shoulder-length, light brown hair, and even, but unremarkable features, and the willowy build of those disinterested in food.

She obviously intended to distract me, because she chatted, even though she had that reserved air about her of the type who would not enjoy being chatty with strangers. She told me her name was Jessica Winton, and that she was from a small town in Canada, where she owned a bookstore named, adorably, The Book and Cranny.

"Difficult to compete with the online giants," I commented.

"Not really," she said, "because my view is that a bookstore is no longer just about selling books. If anything, the online world is creating an even deeper need for connection."

She went on to say that people thought brick-and-mortar bookstores were going to go the way of the dinosaur, but she disagreed. She felt bookstores needed to reinvent themselves as the hub of the community.

I could see she did have a gift for connection, because I felt connected just talking to her. I could also see that she was an astute business-woman, and she reminded me, just a bit, of my younger self. She had succeeded in taking my mind off both my missing dog and my throbbing ankle.

I indulged my curiosity about her. "Do you travel a great deal?"

She gave a little self-deprecating snort. She told me she had never traveled abroad before, and that this was her first real adventure. She said that all her previous adventures had been between the covers, and then added *of books* and gave a little laugh. I could tell, even as distracted and panicky as I was about poor Max, that her adventure might not be turning out exactly as planned.

"Is that man your boyfriend?" I asked, putting unnecessary emphasis on *that*. One of the few perks of being old is you can be as direct as you want.

Jessica hesitated, and then looked uncomfortable. "We've been back and forth online for nearly a year. This is our first actual time together. I thought…"

She let her sentence drift off, but I'm afraid I could tell exactly what she thought, poor thing.

With an ocean between them, and his rather stellar good looks, she had thought he was her Prince Charming.

I had nearly finished the tea, and despite how much I might have enjoyed my companion in other circumstances, I felt deflated and exhausted, and as if I needed to go back to my hotel room, to the inevitable finger-shaking of my head of security, and to begin to mourn the loss of my beloved Max.

But just as I had given up hope, that girl who had put her ticket in her pocket emerged from the crowd, and she was with another girl. They could have been sisters, they looked so much alike with that spiky, very short hair, and both of them with petite builds.

The other girl's hair was lighter, and she had freckles, and it was she who had a squirming

Max held firmly in her arms. Both the young women were laughing, and they looked so vivacious and full of life. It was such a beautiful thing to see—plus the miracle of Max being returned to me—that I started to cry all over again.

I suddenly found Max in my arms. The little monkey—his outfit utterly destroyed—licked my face as though he had not deliberately run away and was delighted to see me. The two young women who looked like sisters introduced themselves. The British girl was Daisy, which is a name I find very old-fashioned and completely lovely.

It turned out the third girl—her name was Aubrey and she was Australian—had scooped up the loose dog as he had continued his mad dash through the crowd. How appropriate is that, that my little joey had been snagged by an Australian? That girl had a "life of the party" way about her.

And then Daisy had come upon her as Aubrey stood there, not quite sure what to do with her find, and brought her—and darling Max—back to me.

We ordered tea all the way around, and I found

out a bit about each of them. Daisy was, indeed, a budding musician who would be playing some of the minor stages at the festival. Aubrey, despite being so outgoing, had something faintly fragile about her, that made me feel concerned about illness. She was involved in some kind of custom painting family business with her brothers. She sounded less than enthused.

I was enjoying visiting with those young women so much I nearly overlooked the fact I was keeping them from their concert, which would be starting momentarily.

I gathered Max, and stood to go. The delight of being in the company of all that vigorous youth had been so lovely I had forgotten the injury to my ankle. But when I stood pain shot through it, and I sank back down with a defeated yelp.

I caught sight of *that* man, Ralph, on the edge of all those moving people, craning his head, obviously looking for Jessica. He saw her and came to the table, casting a terrible shadow on it.

"I see the dog has been found," he said tightly, not at all humbled by the fact there was a *real* dog. He was obviously more than annoyed that his time had been wasted in the search, and that he was about to miss Carlene's show. "Jessica, let's go."

She tilted her chin at him, and I was happy to see a spark of pure fire in those soft, dark eyes.

"Actually, my friend is going to need some help getting home. She's hurt her ankle."

I could have protested that I did not need help, but it really seemed far more important to see how this played out.

"We're missing the concert," he said.

"Yes, we are," she returned, calmly.

"These other women can help her."

"So our enjoyment of the concert is more important than theirs?"

The other two girls sat, wide-eyed, eyes going back and forth, as if they had front row seats at Wimbledon.

Ralph drew in his breath, gave Jessica a withering look and stalked off in the direction of the stadium.

It seemed like all of us had been holding our breath.

"Well," Aubrey said, breaking the silence. "What an ass."

And then we were all giggling like schoolgirls. It made me feel a part of things, something

I certainly had never felt when I was an actual schoolgirl.

"I can manage," I said. "Please go enjoy the concert."

"I don't see how you can manage, at all," Aubrey decided. "I'm going to go see if I can flag down one of those golf cart things that are driving around."

The lady who was running the tea stand came out to collect dishes and I ordered a crumpet for my dear little Max.

The lady brought Max his treat and said, "I'm going to close up now, if you don't need anything else?"

I looked at her and realized she looked exhausted, and also, of course, I knew exactly what she needed.

She needed to feel like everyone else in the park tonight, as if life could have some happy bits in it, and things to look forward to, not just be a sea of endless drudgery.

"Here," I told her. "I don't have any need for this."

I gave her my ticket for the Carlene concert.

Jessica said, "If you've got a friend who can come on short notice, you can have mine, too."

And then Daisy chimed in, and the waitress was suddenly holding three tickets to Carlene. The weariness evaporated from her face and she stared at the tickets as if they had fallen straight from heaven.

"My kids were dying to go. We live close. They can be here in a blink. These tickets are impossible to get," she breathed.

"Nothing is impossible," I told her sternly. She looked hopeful, as the evidence of that very thing was resting in her hand.

Daisy was smiling at me. "I like that. Nothing is impossible."

"But you could still have gone! I don't need all three of you to miss the concert!" I told her, but she was watching that waitress, and I could tell she would not have traded anything for the look on that woman's face. In a world where "self" seems to reign, how had I been lucky enough to run into these three women?

A golf cart came careening down the path, Aubrey in the front with a young man who had on a first aid attendant uniform.

He grabbed a bag, and peeled off my sock and shoe, and poked and prodded at my ankle.

"I think it might be broken," he said. He took

a radio off his belt and, ignoring my protests, ordered an ambulance to meet us at one of the exits.

Even when I insisted, my angels, bless their hearts, refused to leave me, even Aubrey, who still had her ticket.

"What will happen to Max at the emergency room?" Daisy asked, practically. "No, we'll come and take turns staying outside with him until you're released."

And so, we all ended up in the golf cart, though it hilariously overloaded it.

Aubrey said, "I feel as if I'm in a carload of clowns heading for the center ring," and we all laughed, and despite my ankle throbbing, that golf cart ride through Faelledparken felt very spontaneous and joyous. There was an ambulance waiting at the exit, manned by two swoonworthy Danish men. Jessica came in the ambulance with me, and Aubrey and Daisy followed with Max in a cab.

Hours later, outside the hospital, with my ankle bandaged—thankfully just severely bruised, not broken—we exchanged hugs. We were beaming at each other as if we had known one another forever, the most delicious little bond between us, the kind that only a closely averted catastrophe can create.

Finally, I was able to look at the young women who had put their own agendas so selflessly aside to help me.

Really look at them.

I've had this unusual gift since I was a child.

My mother was appalled by it and called me *fey*. She went as far as to discourage my use of it by saying she thought maybe I wasn't a *real* Ascot, after all, but an Irish traveler baby, fallen off the caravan.

I'm afraid the thought of *really* being an Irish traveler, instead of a member of a very stuffy aristocratic family, bound by rules and customs and most especially by *what will people think*, gave me many fantastic hours of make-believe and much needed respite from my mother.

I certainly wasn't fey in the way most people would think of that. I was unable to speak to dead people, an enviable talent that has become so popular there are now entire television programs about it.

It was just that I could look at people and sense what they needed.

In my younger years, it had been quite overwhelming, especially in a crowd. People's needs, both large and small, swarmed around me like restless bees, buzzing...

She needs to see a doctor...he needs a long walk in the forest...he needs glasses...she needs a new life...he needs a new wife...

As I had gotten older I'd learned to keep my observations mostly to myself. People didn't really appreciate a complete stranger approaching them with life advice. I'd also gotten better at shutting off some of it, and had learned that knowing what someone needed—even when sometimes they did not know themselves—gave me quite a sharp advantage in business.

Looking at my rescuers right now, I knew with startling clarity exactly what each of them needed.

Still, you didn't attain the incredible successes in business that I had, by relying on your instincts alone.

"I have ordered a car for Max and me. I'll make my way back to my hotel." Jessica was going to protest, but she had done enough for me, so I held up my hand. "But I would so love to keep in touch. I'm brand-new to social media. Would you mind if..."

Of course they saw me as entirely adorable, and wrote their full names and all their social media contact information—Facebook and Twitter and Instagram—on a scrap of paper I provided. They had already exchanged information with each other, but they had put that directly into their phones. No scraps of paper for their generation.

Having all that information meant I could spy on their private lives shamelessly—young people were so oblivious to who was watching what they revealed online—to confirm if what I thought they needed *really* was what they needed.

And then, I was in the unique position of being able to give it to them. I felt no rush, at all. They were young, and at that age where their needs could change in a heartbeat. I would be patient. Bide my time. Wait until I was 100 percent certain.

I realized, gleefully, all the girls had accepted me introducing myself simply as Viv, and not one of them had any idea who I really was— Vivian Ascot, one of the sponsors of the music festival and CEO of one of the largest and oldest corporations in the world.

"What a good little boy you've been," I told

Max. "You've brought me this wonderful opportunity."

I watched the girls walk away, arm in arm, lifelong friendships appeared to be budding. Jessica was going to stay with Aubrey tonight instead of running the risk of running into Ralph at her hotel, and then they were all planning to go together to watch Daisy's "gig" at the festival the next day. I contemplated what those young women, my rescuers, needed. They were so young. So filled with hope. So confident that they knew everything they wanted and needed for happiness. Naturally, they had no idea.

Of the three of them, I had gotten to know Jessica the most. I loved the way she had described Timber Falls, the small resort town in the Canadian Rockies where she had grown up and ran her bookstore, and where her parents still lived.

But, while it had sounded like a great place for aging parents, and possibly for a short holiday, and while Jessica undoubtedly felt safe there, what longing had led her to Copenhagen? Whatever she had told herself, I felt her journey to the music festival was not so much about a romance as it was about a longing for a larger world. Young people need challenges to make life seem fresh and interesting.

The small town had to be quite stifling for someone so smart and ambitious. And single. But now, after the Ralph fiasco, it seemed there was a possibility Jessica would go back there and be more reluctant than ever to explore all life had to offer.

Well, not if I had anything to do with it.

Waiting for my car to come, I felt the most delicious wave of happiness. I decided playing fairy godmother to those three young women was probably going to be just about the most fun I had ever had.

CHAPTER ONE

JESSICA WINTON STEPPED out through the Customs and Immigration doors into the full flurry of the arrival area of John F. Kennedy International Airport. Her hand tightened on the handle of her wheeled carry-on.

She had not seen a crowd like this since that summer night of the music festival in Copenhagen. Could that be two years ago, already?

Yes, almost to the day.

And look at how that had turned out: her grand virtual romance had been exposed as horribly naive and shabby when the harsh light of reality had shone on it.

This was going to be more of the same. Jessica could just feel it. Yes, there it was, the panicky sensation rising in her chest.

What moment of madness had made me agree to this?

Right now it felt as if, after that initial glance, it would have been better—so much better—if she had just junked the email that had brought her to New York City as one of those endless variations of the Nigerian orphaned princess scam.

Dream job this time. Dream man last time. Did she always have to be the sucker for a dream?

She cast a desperate glance back at the doors that had just whispered closed behind her, but saw that reentering the Customs area was strictly forbidden. What would she do if she managed to go back through the doors, anyway? Demand to be sent home, like a child who had found summer camp not to her liking?

She'd been invited to a job interview here in New York City. Of course, she already knew she couldn't take it. Even if it was her dream job, which it most definitely was. She had her life and it was a totally satisfactory life. She was successful, she was a respected member of the community. Who was always the keynote speaker at Career Day at the Timber Falls High School?

No, a job in New York City, at this point in her life, was out of the question.

And yet, here she stood, as if pulled by an invisible cable. She'd been up front with the marketing firm Jensen, Henry and Ascot that she wasn't in a position to take the job. But they had been persuasive. Why not just come? Have the initial discussion? See some of New York City? And then, an airline ticket, and a reservation confirmation for three days at a posh Manhattan hotel had been sent, as if that was all settled.

No one could say no to that. Could they?

And yet, standing here, exhausted—it took longer to travel from Timber Falls than the time she would spend in Manhattan—and not quite knowing what do next, Jess felt regret at being so impulsive. It never paid off for her. Other people could embrace spontaneity, but it seemed as if it just wasn't a good fit for her.

Something wasn't ringing true about all this and she should have paid attention to that feeling instead of being persuaded by Aubrey's ever chipper Australian voice coming over the line, chiding her.

Is something not ringing true, or do you just believe good things can't happen to you?

Daisy, while pleased that Jessica had decided to accept the trip to New York, had said rather gleefully, *Looking at a new job is like going to the pet store and looking at puppies. You're al-*

ready partway committed to taking one home with you.

What if it proved harder to resist the temptation than Jessica anticipated?

It wasn't going to be that hard to resist if her first few minutes in New York were any indication. The Customs lineup had been slow, the official had been unnervingly unfriendly and, now that she had been admitted to the country, the crowds were crushing, and her stomach was growling. And as far as she could see, there was no one here to greet her.

Her tablet case and her purse were strapped securely to the pull handle of her carry-on bag. She turned to it. She fished the piece of paper from the outside pocket of her purse and looked at it.

The letter instructed her she would be met at the airport by James Gilbert-Cooper, Chief Operating Officer of Jensen, Henry and Ascot, a marketing firm that had a division that exclusively handled bookstores. The man could potentially be her new boss!

But not if this was his idea of making a good first impression. Leaving her hanging.

It's been two minutes, Jessica chided herself. She forced a deep breath, and a change in attitude. She was sure Aubrey, her irrepressible Australian friend, would invite her to turn it all into a game.

Okay. What would someone with a name like that look like? Old, she decided. And very proper. A vested suit and a bow tie. Definitely glasses. Round-framed ones.

Jessica looked around nervously. She couldn't see anyone who looked like she expected Mr. Gilbert-Cooper to look.

What if he didn't come? Should she wait? Call the number on the letter? Surely the office would be closed. Should she take a cab to the hotel she had the reservation at? Didn't cabdrivers take advantage of people like her? Despite her best effort to look sophisticated, Jessica felt she was probably telegraphing that she was from a different country and a small town. Did cabdrivers have to pass some kind of test of their driving skills? What if she was killed in traffic? And what about their character? What if she was driven to a remote location and—

Stop it! Jess ordered herself.

She made herself think of Aubrey and Daisy, and the wonderful connection the three of them had enjoyed since Copenhagen—thank you very much, WhatsApp. Both women had encouraged her to come, and hinted that maybe they thought Jess tended to play it too safe, and make her world too small. It was funny what close friends they had all become, despite the fact they came from different parts of the globe and had very different lifestyles. Still, Jessica confided things to them that she would not have dreamed of saying to any of the people she shared a life with on a daily basis.

Take a chance, Aubrey had insisted after Jess had received the intriguing email and determined it was not a hoax.

Too late, Jess was remembering almost those exact same words—from other well-meaning friends—had led her to the disaster in Copenhagen with Ralph.

Jessica took a deep breath, and searched the sea of faces waiting in the arrivals area. None of them seemed to fit her idea of James Gilbert-Cooper, and none of them seemed particularly interested in her.

I'll be wearing a red jacket.

Thinking about it now, that could be left open to some interpretation. The jacket in question leaned toward burgundy. She should have been more descriptive: the color was like sun filtering through a bottle of merlot, which was what she had thought when she splurged on it.

Why hadn't she thought out the intricacies of being met by a stranger in such a large airport a little more thoroughly? Had she been expecting someone to be waving a sign with her name on it?

To be perfectly honest, yes, she had.

And then she saw him.

It felt as if the sea of people around her had been storm-stirred waves that suddenly went still.

He was standing, leaning one shoulder, casually, against a post, long legs crossed at the ankle. Unlike almost everyone else in the terminal, he seemed to be neither waiting eagerly for someone nor rushing off somewhere.

He seemed, while not exactly indifferent to the controlled chaos around him, above it, somehow, untouched by it.

He was wearing a suit of the lightest charcoal gray, the jacket open, the cut showed off both his broad shoulders and the length of those powerful legs. The shirt was a crisp white, a tie, in an

unlikely shade of pale pink, was knotted somewhat carelessly at his throat. Jessica's gaze rested
on his shoes—leather, buffed to a soft sheen, a
shade of tan that shouldn't have worked with the
suit, but did.

Not one man in all of her hometown of Timber
Falls could carry off any shade of pink, in any
circumstances, and certainly not in combination
with those shoes. The man's sophistication—his
absolute confidence—was underscored by the
color of his hair.

It was gray—*not fifty shades,* Jessica scolded
herself—but certainly a dozen, from several startling variations of silver, to strands of white, and
tiny hints of black. Rather than aging him in any
way, his hair, and the superb cut of it, made him
seem distinguished, in control and fabulously
sure of himself.

He was scrolling through his phone, and she
had a ridiculous desire to know what was holding his interest like that.

Photos? Of his children? He somehow did not
look the type. Wife? No ring on his finger. Girl-
friend? Ah, probably plenty of those.

He glanced up, as if he'd sensed her gaze on
him. Jessica saw his eyes were darker than her

own, coffee as compared to chocolate, and his gaze was intense, and stripping.

Embarrassed by feeling such a pull to a complete stranger, Jess looked quickly away and scanned the crowd for the far more dowdy Gilbert-Cooper of her imagination. When she didn't see anyone, she cast another longing glance over her shoulder at the firmly closed Customs doors behind her.

And then, disgusted with herself for the weakness, Jessica found she could not resist glancing back at that man one more time. He was scanning the crowds now. She noted his brow was furrowed in a frown, almost as if he was irritated. And then it appeared he saw whomever he was looking for because he tucked his phone away, and moved. Straight toward her! She could feel herself holding her breath.

Jessica didn't know if she was relieved or sorry when he stopped in front of the woman beside her.

Who happened to be wearing a red jacket.

Paired with a rather hideous flowered skirt.

With jet-black beehive hair and too much makeup.

"Jessica Winton?" he asked the woman.

Jessica felt the insult of it, and also her wariness increased. Was that how he pictured a small-town bookstore owner, then? If that was the case, why had his company gone to such lengths to get her to come?

Still, the inquiry did mean that *he* was Gilbert-Cooper. Her potential boss!

"Honey," the woman said, eyeing him as if he was a hot fudge sundae on a sultry July day, "I'll be whoever you want me to be."

Jessica understood the polite thing to do would be to go correct this, but some little devil made her want to see him pay the price for his misconception.

"I believe it would be a yes or no answer," he said after a pause. "Jessica Winton?"

The woman extended her hand. "And you are?"

Jessica's mouth fell open. Was this stranger beside her really going to pretend to be *her?*

It obviously was time to say something, she knew that. But she was inappropriately tickled to watch Mr. Suave and Confident's hand disappear inside a ham-like grip. The woman didn't let go, either. In fact she blinked, eyelashes so heavy with mascara that it looked like she had spiders glued on, at him.

He extricated his hand with difficulty. "Jamie Gilbert-Cooper."

If they had said Jamie, instead of James, in the letter, Jessica might have been better prepared for him. She would have been prepared to meet the hero of *Outlander* not someone dowdy and old and in a bow tie! Still, she was guiltily aware she had let this go far enough.

"I don't see a wedding ring," the woman said boldly. "A guy like you not hitched?"

His discomfort was acute, and really Jessica could not have him believing for another second that this woman was *her*.

Well, maybe one more second. Just until she heard his answer.

"Not *hitched*," he said, only the tiniest tightness in his tone indicating he was irritated, "and not planning on it, either."

"Well, that makes you exactly my kinda guy, Mr. Gilbert-Cooper."

Jessica cleared her throat. "Did you say Gilbert-Cooper? That's who I'm waiting for."

Jessica looked at them both innocently, as if she had just noticed them.

The woman swiveled her head, and gave her a glare as if Jessica was an uninvited guest at a private party. Then she turned back to Jamie Gilbert-Cooper. "Honey, you are one long, tall drink of handsome. You can't fault a girl for trying. Can you?"

Apparently an answer was required.

He did not look like he was caught off balance often, but he definitely was now. Casting Jessica a faintly accusing look, he muttered, "Enjoy your stay in New York."

"I'm here for the Gidgets Widgets Convention," she said, not so easily dismissed. She fished in a large red handbag that missed matching her jacket by a shade or two, and handed him a card. "I'm Debbie, a sales consultant."

He glanced at the card and actually blanched before quickly handing it back to her.

She pouted prettily, cast Jessica another dark look. "Now you look like a gal who could benefit from—" she held out the card that he had returned to her.

He intercepted quickly. "No," he said, with such firmness even Debbie was dissuaded. Miffed, she put her card back in her purse and then marched off through the crowds.

"Your loss," she called over her ample shoulder, before disappearing from view.

"What is a Gidgets Widget?" Jessica asked, watching her go, trying to contain her glee at his discomfort.

"You don't want to know," he told her firmly. He turned his attention back to her. "So you are the real Jessica Winton, then?"

"Guilty."

"It seems to me you might have stepped in sooner."

"Um…"

"You enjoyed that."

"Just eager to clear up misconceptions about small-town bookstore owners everywhere." *Potential boss*, she reminded herself sternly. Even if she pretty much had already decided she was not taking this job, she needed to be professional.

Her potential boss cocked his head and studied her. He was much taller than her. Close up, the chiseled perfection of his features was even more evident. He had the faintest hint of gray-and-black stubble on his face. Deliberate, obviously. Sexually potent, terribly.

The most subtle fragrance came off him, faintly spicy, faintly exotic and strongly masculine.

"It was the red jacket, not any kind of preconceived conception about small towns or book-store owners."

His voice was as smooth and smoky as the twenty-one-year-old Glenfiddich her father broke out once a year at Christmastime. She did not think she wanted to be having a conversation with him that included the word *conception*, no matter what the circumstances.

She had worn the red jacket that she had purchased for her trip to Copenhagen two years ago. It was, easily, the best item of clothing that she owned, the only time she had ever splurged on a designer name.

But suddenly she was *so* aware it was two years old, and it didn't feel as timeless as she had told herself it would be when she had indulged her desire for it. Her blouse felt wrinkled and her black pants felt travel-rumpled. For the first time in her life, she felt aware of the importance of shoes, and sorry that she had chosen the loafers she had on for their comfort and practicality.

Meeting a man like this, one wanted to have on four-inch heels.

Jessica Winton, she chided herself, *you've never had on four-inch heels in your life!*

She'd been concentrating on how to look businesslike this morning as she had prepared for the flight, and so her hair was held back in a clip, and her makeup was minimal.

"Jamie," he introduced himself to her, as if she wasn't already 100 percent aware of who he was! His voice was deep and had an entirely too sensual rasp to it. "Gilbert-Cooper."

She let loose the handle of her suitcase. Her fingers actually felt cramped from holding it so tight, and she extended her hand to him.

"How do you do?" she said, and then could have kicked herself for how ridiculously formal and stilted she sounded.

He took her hand.

The feeling of stillness, of all that activity around her fading to nothing, increased. His handshake was firm, strong and sexy.

How could a handshake be sexy?

"Mr. Cooper. Mr. Cooper!"

He let go of her hand, and turned, frowning. Jessica could see Debbie, the Gidgets Widgets gal, steaming back toward them.

"I forgot to give you the free sample!" she bellowed. She was coming at them brandishing something that looked like a large green cucumber. People were staring at her, startled and wary.

Jamie actually tucked Jessica behind him, putting his body between her and the charging saleslady. There was something so entirely protective about it that it could completely dissolve that potential boss barrier.

Jessica felt, more than saw, a movement out of the corner of her eye. Someone jostled her. Hard. She lurched into Jamie's back, and he took a startled step forward then turned around.

"Hey!" Jamie cried.

She realized, stunned, someone had grabbed her suitcase. As she watched, frozen in horror, what appeared to be a businessman—nearly as well dressed as Jamie himself—darted through the crowds with her suitcase, her purse and tablet case still attached to the handle. He wasn't running, just moving fast, like someone late for a connection.

"He stole my things!"

Jamie took both her shoulders in a strong grip and scanned her face. The strength in his touch, the calm in those dark eyes—he had thick sooty eyelashes that the women of the world would die for—had a way of making the calamity unfolding fade into a distant background.

"You're all right?"

As soon as she nodded, he released her shoulders and took off at a dead run after the perpetrator.

Even with it being such an awful moment, some despicable part of herself insisted on noting how athletic he was, and insisted on seeing this as somehow intensely romantic. She would have to share this story with the romance genre fans who met at the bookstore once a month. The members of the Smitten Word would be delighted! And so would Aubrey and Daisy. They had told her life could be full of unexpected adventures, and here you had it. She had been in New York less than fifteen minutes, and she was being rescued by a stunning hero.

Not that she should be thinking about her potential boss like that. It was highly inappropriate.

It occurred to her, almost peripherally, that Debbie had disappeared. That seemed impossible. She had been charging straight toward them. How did someone that size, that colorfully dressed and that loud, simply vanish?

Without the calming effect of Jamie's touch and gaze, Jessica could feel the full implication of the theft. She felt rattled and off balance.

She took a deep breath, then found an uncomfortable seat.

Jamie was just the kind of man you could rely on in a situation like this, she told herself. He radiated an ability to control the world. He would catch the perpetrator, return her belongings to her and the ice would be broken between them. He would forgive her for having not stepped in sooner to reveal Debbie as an imposter, and she would choose to believe that it was the red jacket that had caused the mistaken identity, and not a stereotypical idea of what a female business owner from a tiny dot on the map in the Canadian Rockies would look like.

In a few minutes they would be sitting in a cab—or maybe he had an extraordinary car—but either way, they would be laughing about her introduction to the city. She could picture those firm, sensual lips tilted with laughter, the dark eyes sparking, and that picture made a very improper shiver run up and down her spine.

She craned her neck to see, but the crowds had swallowed up both Jamie and the thief making off with her suitcase.

Seconds ticked by, and then minutes.

Finally, she saw Jamie coming back through

the crowds toward her. She leaped to her feet but her relief at seeing the only face she knew in all of New York was short-lived.

His hands were empty and there was a look like thunder on his handsome face. He was breathing hard.

Reality collided with fantasy. As he approached her, he loosened his tie with one hand, and held his phone to his ear with the other. Obviously he was talking to the police or airport security.

It occurred to Jessica that instead of mooning about, making up stories, she should have been calling the authorities. They could have been setting up traps at the exits, watching security cameras…

Except her phone was in her purse.

He ended his call as he came back to her. "I'm sorry," he said, running an agitated hand through the multicolored gray silk of his hair. "He's obviously very skilled at this. The Artful Dodger. I couldn't catch him. I lost him in the crowds. He probably has some favorite getaway route, and some little hole he ducks into."

She could feel the tiniest prick of impending tears behind her eyes. She would not be a country bumpkin in front of this super sophisticated suave man. She would not! But the enormity of what had happened was hitting her. Hard.

It wasn't an adventure. It was a catastrophe. Trust her to mix the two things up!

"I called the police," Jamie said, his voice soothing, despite the anger on his face. "Unfortunately, there are nearly two hundred claims a day of baggage theft at this airport."

"Two hundred thefts a day?" she gasped. So much for a team of people scanning the exits and the security cameras in search of *her* stolen items.

"Most of the stuff is grabbed from the luggage carousels, but there's been quite a sophisticated ring operating lately. Teams. One distracts, one grabs the goods."

He lifted an elegant shoulder in apology.

"In Timber Falls," she said, "we probably don't have two dozen thefts in a whole year. I've had two shoplifting incidents in the four years that I've had had my bookstore. Poor Mrs. Webber, who was getting dementia, and Sonny McGill, a teenage boy who had been going through a rebel-without-a-cause phase."

She realized she was babbling nervously. She realized she had probably revealed all kinds of things about her life that he would find quaint and amusing.

On the other hand, maybe she didn't have to say a word to reveal secrets about herself. The theft team had obviously targeted her as hopelessly small-town from the minute she had come out those doors.

"I'm really sorry," he said. The genuine distress in his voice made the cold, hard reality of what she was dealing with intensify.

"Did they peg me as naive?" she asked softly.

"Hey, don't say that as if it's somehow your fault you were robbed. Honestly, I feel as if I should have twigged in on Debbie's over-the-top performance." He turned his attention back to his phone. "As I suspected. No Gidgets Widgets Convention in New York this weekend." He scowled as he scrolled. "No Gidgets Widgets, period."

"Too bad you didn't keep the business card," she said forlornly.

He raised an eyebrow at her.

"Fingerprints."

"Uh, yeah, I somehow doubt this crime would have rated fingerprinting. Sorry. Apparently, we can file a police report online, though. And we need to get your credit cards looked after. Your phone plan canceled."

We. Because *she* no longer had a computer. It felt somehow insulting that the crime that had been committed against her did not even warrant a face-to-face visit with authorities. His suggestions for dealing with practicalities made her face the grim truth of the matter.

"I'm not getting my things back, am I?"

He looked uncomfortable. "Um—

The prick of tears intensified behind her eyes. "I don't have my phone," she stammered. "And no cash. No clothes."

It occurred to her that her reliance on this formidable specimen of a man, a person she barely knew, and her potential boss, was 100 percent.

It was shocking, and yet her mind insisted on itemizing things of no importance at all.

No makeup. No perfume. No favorite shampoo. No pink frosted nail polish. No novel to escape into.

She glanced one more time at the Customs and Immigration door she had exited from. Even if she could go back through there, she needed proper documentation to go anywhere.

"My passport," she whispered. "How am I

going to get home? How do I go about replacing it?"

Jessica realized she was trapped in New York City. With Jamie Gilbert-Cooper.

Such a dreadful, dreadful mistake to come here.

Just like her ill-advised adventure to Copenhagen.

The noise and activity around her seemed to rise up to almost unbearable levels: the intercom warning people not to leave their luggage unattended, a shout of laughter, the constant hum of busy people moving.

Jessica suddenly longed for the comfort of Timber Falls: for her charming bookstore on Main Street, and for her little cottage in her mom and dad's backyard. She longed for the turquoise waters of the nearby lake, for the cool green of a forest just getting ready to welcome summer. She wished she was sitting beside Timber Falls, that thunderous noise filling her every sense, her face lifted to the spray.

"We'll get it all sorted out," Jamie told her, his voice solid and reassuring.

Something in the utter strength of that voice made her look at him. Really look at him. He was gorgeous, yes, but there was an underlying calm there, a man, who despite all the sophisticated trappings, you would want at your side if the bandits were coming at you with knives in their teeth.

Unfortunately, there was something about his composure, his strength, that allowed her to let hers slip, just a little bit.

She felt her throat close.

And then, even though she ordered herself not to, the first tear slipped out of her eye. And then the second one. And then, the floodgates opened. There. She could be grateful that, in her rush to get the plane this morning, she had not bothered with mascara.

It was of little comfort that James Gilbert-Cooper's colossal self-confidence seemed to evaporate, completely, in the face of her tears.

CHAPTER TWO

"DON'T CRY," JAMIE ordered Jessica Winton, a little more sharply than he intended. The order seemed to have the exact opposite effect of what he had intended. Her face crumpled a little more.

"Please?" he added, trying for a softer tone. Instead, he could hear desperation in his tone. Jamie's father had died when he was eighteen. There had been so many tears from his mother and his sister, so much emotion that he had been powerless to stanch. He *hated* the memories of that period of his life, and couldn't believe he'd been plunged into them by the vulnerability— as understandable as it was—of a complete stranger.

Despite a terrible start, this was still a business association. One of the things he *loved* about business was that it was a black-and-white world. Pesky things like emotions—feelings—could be left safely outside the perimeters of the work environment.

His relief that she was the real Jessica Winton—that he didn't have to spend three days trying to be civil to that obnoxious barge in a dress—was not standing up to the challenge of the stolen luggage. He could handle crass and vulgar over soft and vulnerable any day.

He realized, since the feeling thing had crept in, exactly what he *was* feeling.

Guilt.

He had failed. That barge in a dress had tricked him into letting his guard down, and the woman who had suffered the consequences of his failure was trying not to cry and failing as completely as he had.

Guilt was also a residue of that period in his life when he had been powerless over the pain of those he loved, where he had also felt the agonies of failure.

This, Jamie told himself firmly, has nothing to do with *that*. But as he watched, first one little tear slid over that exquisite cheekbone, and then another, and then those slender shoulders heaved, and the storm came.

He had lied to Jessica Winton. He *had* entertained preconceived notions of what a small-town bookstore owner would look like. Young had not been part of that equation. Neither had completely adorable.

He was not prepared for huge brown eyes the color of melted milk chocolate, the lush fullness of a bottom lip, the little mole on the tiny lobe of her ear.

Of course he was not prepared for any of that! Jessica Winton being offered a job was all part of *the joke's on you.*

Jamie had been part of the internationally renowned marketing firm of Jensen, Henry and Ascot for seven years, the last three of them as the Chief Operating Officer. Until two and a half years ago, he'd been unaware that the Ascot part of the corporation name was anything more than a silent partnership. The Ascot name was, after all, in everything, from nuts to bolts to concert production. He'd been a bit surprised there was an actual person attached to that iconic name.

And what a person. Auntie Mame on steroids.

Vivian, herself, had descended on the office, at a meeting concerning the promotion of the annual Ascot-sponsored music festival. Despite being diminutive, she had been larger than life in oversize Gucci sunglasses, a fur hat unapologetically made of some endangered species and with a fat little sausage dog in a jeweled collar stuffed under her arm.

Jamie thought all her ideas were dreadful, and he might have rolled his eyes at the worst of them: something to do with the name she had come up with for that year's festival to be held in Copenhagen.

She had lifted her sunglasses and cast him a flinty look that could have stripped paint.

"Uh-oh," Phil Jensen had said in an undertone, "she never forgets."

At the time, Jamie had thought Phil was ribbing him. It had been the smallest thing, really, and Jamie had dismissed it within minutes of leaving the meeting.

But fast-forward to a few weeks ago, and there he was called into Phil's office. Vivian Ascot, whom he had never seen or even heard of since that day, had resurfaced, not in person, but in the form of an order.

Apparently, she had discovered some small-town bookstore owner whom she thought would be ideal for representing some of JHA's publishing, author and bookstore accounts.

Bookstores were a tricky marketing business these days, but apparently an independent owner had caught Vivian's attention by making her tiny town bookstore extremely viable, by making it, according to the letter Phil had read from, *the hub of the community.*

No matter that the publishing and bookstore accounts were Jamie's particular cup of tea, or that one of his genuine delights was working with authors. Miss Winton was being offered a job opportunity, sight unseen, and she wasn't to know Vivian Ascot was behind it.

And what's more, Ms. Ascot-Who-Never-Forgot, had specifically requested that Jamie be enlisted in the recruitment of Miss Winton.

"We're supposed to seduce her," Phil had said, dryly. "And that's a quote."

"Like some small-town bookstore owner wouldn't jump for joy at this opportunity?"

"Uh, my initial contact would make it seem like Ms. Winton is not exactly jumping. I'm not prepared to risk Vivian Ascot's displeasure. But it's more than that. Before you came on board here, we had hit a bit of a bump in the business road. Viv bailed us out. Failure is not an option."

We're supposed to seduce her. That had seemed like a very casual term of reference a few days ago.

Not so much now with Jessica Winton standing in front of him, crying.

She really could be a poster child for the small-town girl with her undyed hair pulled primly back, her basically makeup-free face, her guileless expression.

Despite the red jacket—he thought if it had been called burgundy the barge mix-up could have been avoided—there was something very understated about her. He moved in a world where people, and particularly women, drew attention *to* their assets, not away from them.

She had, he could see, a beautiful figure, and yet if he was to describe her look, he might call it *spinster librarian.* She'd probably be hurt to know it was *exactly* the look, had he not been distracted, that he would have assigned to a small-town bookstore owner, though one who was twenty years older than her.

Her expression was one of pure vulnerability: those huge dark tear-filled eyes, her thick lashes studded with diamond tears, the trembling of an unexpectedly tempting mouth.

Everything about her—except maybe that mouth—said wholesome. Fresh. Untainted. Easily hurt.

Which had made her a pretty natural mark for the likes of Debbie and the Gidgets Widgets team, unfortunately.

"It's going to be okay," he said and felt something he rarely felt: clumsily inept.

Not unsurprisingly, she was not at all reassured. He recalled he might have used that same expression *often* in that terrible year after his father had died, and his sister and his mother had not been reassured then either.

Jessica buried her face in her hands and wept. He froze.

Do something, he snapped at himself.

What? a voice asked back.

Anything.

So, he patted her shoulder. The curve of it was so delicate that it felt as if he had whacked her. He withdrew his hand hastily. She hiccuped noisily. People were glancing at her. And then at him. As if he was supposed to know what to do.

He wanted to protest. *She's a job candidate, not a love interest.*

He ordered himself to back off and let her have her cry. It was not unnatural for her to be crying. She was ten minutes into her visit to one of the largest and most sophisticated cities in the world, and she'd been robbed.

"I'm sorry," he said, "I know it's a nasty turn of events."

The wrong thing to say—no surprise, underscoring what he had already deduced, great businessman and emotional moron that he was—as her sobs, muffled by her hands, became louder.

"It's going to be okay," he repeated, even though those very words had had no effect on any of the many occasions he had used them.

It occurred to him words—or at least not any he could think of—were simply not going to cut it.

To his own shock, some instinct moved him closer to her, instead of farther away. To his own shock, he tugged her hands from her face, scanned her tearstained cheeks, and then, with a sigh, folded his arms around her, and pulled her to him.

She did not resist, but snuggled into him like a wet kitten rescued from a storm. Nothing could have prepared him for that, either: the softness of her, the warmth of her, the way she was making him feel, well, manly, in a way he was not sure he had ever experienced before.

She sobbed against his chest, her tears leaving a warm patch that was threatening to melt even his ever cynical heart.

He could smell a heady scent coming off her hair, which was tickling the bottom of his chin. What was that? Lavender? Since when did he know what lavender smelled like? And yet it seemed as if he could picture a field full of those tall purple blooms, with her walking through it, her hand grazing the top of the flowers like a blessing.

He gave himself a mental shake and wondered if he should say something to hurry this along before he ended up picturing himself in that field of lavender with her.

There, there seemed too grandfatherly. *Pull yourself together* seemed too hard and *I understand how you're feeling* would have been a stretch.

After what seemed to be at least an hour, the length between the sobs—he was timing them, though he thought that was probably supposed to be for contractions—lengthened and then lengthened a little more, until they stopped and she drew in a long, shuddering sigh.

Finally, she stepped away from him.

His eyes went to one of the airport clocks. Three minutes, not an hour. He looked back at her. Her face was blotchy, her hair was mussed and the front of her blouse, where it had been pressed against him, was creased. Three minutes of crying could cause quite a look of dishevelment in a woman!

"Thanks. I'm sorry." She looked mortified with herself. She gazed in the region of the wet blotches on his shirt, appalled, and then said, again, "I'm sorry."

"Don't be."

"I'm tired. And I'm hungry. And basically, I'm a mess. How do you like me, so far?"

Thankfully, she did not seem to be waiting for an answer, because the truth was, he did find her oddly appealing at the same time that he did not think she was cut out for the high-pressure world of JHA.

It was harsh judgment, but there it was. Despite the fact he was supposed to seduce her to take the job, he could feel himself planning the exact opposite. He'd show her around the city, as per plan, gently dissuade her from a career at JHA, then put her back on a plane as soon as they got her passport sorted out. He'd announce his failure to the powers that be, and then get on with his life as if she had never happened.

It occurred to Jamie, with just a bit of shock, that maybe it wasn't all about her. That maybe he felt a need to protect himself from this small-town girl and the things she could coax out of him without half trying.

She sniffed. "I don't even have a tissue."

He wasn't sure if she wanted the tissue for her little red nose, or to try to repair the damage to his shirt.

"I don't even have a tissue," she repeated. The issue of the tissue as a sign of her complete destitution seemed as if it might push her over the edge again, so Jamie hurriedly pulled the pocket square from his suit and handed it to her.

Thankfully, she dabbed delicately at her nose and left the front of his shirt alone. She had a very cute nose, small and a little turned up at the end. Her bottom lip was trembling a bit, and it was more than cute. Full and plump. Jamie gave himself an annoyed mental shake.

Even though he was determined she would never work for him, a little propriety was in order. Which meant not trying to guess what those lips would taste like.

She was vulnerable. He did not take advantage of the vulnerable. Or sweet girls from small towns.

Embracing her had been a mistake—visions of lavender fields proof of that—but it was one he now intended to quickly rectify.

"Let's get you settled," he said, his voice a touch on the curt side, more to remind himself than her of the nature of their relationship. "I have a car outside."

She stepped out the doors with him, and flinched as they were plunged into even more madness; horns honking, tires squealing, the smell of hot engines on a summer night.

"It's dark already," she said.

He glanced at his phone. "Ten p.m."

She nodded. "I'd forgotten. A three-hour time difference."

JHA had several cars and drivers at their disposal, but when the uniformed driver held open the door of the Bentley for Jessica, she took in the well-appointed opulence inside the vehicle with little pleasure. In fact, she seemed to sink even a little more into herself. By the time he got in the other door, she was squished up against her own door and staring straight ahead. She looked very pale. And fragile. She was clutching his pocket square as if it was a lifeline.

The car pulled away from the curb, and headed for the Grand Central Parkway, Jamie realized he needed to take charge of this situation.

"We've got a forty-minute drive into Manhattan. Let's make use of it and get you started on canceling credit cards and your phone," he suggested, and pulled his tablet from a pouch in the door. "Maybe contact your bank about emergency funds. You can use this, and I'll make some calls to see what the procedure is to have your passport reported missing and then replaced."

He quickly put in his password and handed her the open tablet. He was entering his comfort zone—take action—but she was staring numbly at the computer on her lap.

"Bring up your credit card company," he directed her, and then plunged into his own calls. He covered the phone with his hand for a moment. "Maybe try the chat feature if they have one."

When he disconnected from his calls, she had closed the computer.

"The bank's website had a number I can call

tomorrow about emergency funds. Meanwhile, the cards are canceled," she reported, "and my phone. Thank you for realizing how important that was. I think I'm so shaken, I would have overlooked that and had a billion-dollar phone bill to who knows where on top of everything else."

"Great." He ticked off their accomplishments on his fingers. "Credit cards canceled. Phone canceled. We'll work on your bank and the passport tomorrow. The Canadian Consulate isn't open right now, but we'll go see them first thing in the morning. From what I could tell, it looks as though there is a procedure for issuing emergency travel documents or a temporary passport."

"Thank you, again, for taking charge."

He smiled at her, the kind of reassuring smile, he hoped, that said, *See? No more tears are necessary.* "I'm in the zone. Solving problems is my specialty. So moving on, are you up to tackling the police report?"

"I'm sorry, no."

He lifted an eyebrow at her. A more sophisticated companion would have gotten it: *I'm trying to take your mind off things. Play along. Don't make it any more awkward than it already is.*

But she shook her head. "I'm exhausted. I've been traveling for two days. Timber Falls is not close to a major airport. You have to drive for a day to get to one. And then I chose a hotel close to the airport, and couldn't sleep for planes and sirens and noise. And then, this."

See? It was going to get awkward. That luscious bottom lip was trembling again.

"I should have never let go of my suitcase handle. What was I thinking? What kind of idiot lets their guard down in New York City?"

He wanted to tell her the crime rate in the city had been dropping since the 1990s and it was now considered one of the safest large cities in the United States, but it seemed she might not appreciate that insight at the moment.

"Would it be a mugging, would you say?" she asked. "I mean, I guess I would assume some violence in a mugging. It felt violent. He did push me."

"Are you hurt?" The hospital! Good grief, here he was looking after all the business details, solving problems, and she was in need of medical assistance. It made Jamie realize, surprised, that he might be feeling a little more off balance than he was prepared to let on. To her, and even more, to himself.

"Oh, no, I'm not hurt physically. Just shaken. Badly."

She held out her hand. He could see it was trembling like a leaf in a breeze. Without asking her, and propriety be damned, Jamie pushed a built-in panel in the back of the driver's seat that opened a minibar. He poured her a generous cognac and handed it to her.

For a moment she stared at it silently, as if she planned to refuse. Then she grabbed it, took a sip, wrinkled her nose and then tossed the whole thing back.

She shuddered, from her toes to her head, then held out the glass.

Clearly, she wanted more. Clearly, that would be a dumb idea. Still, her hand had stopped shaking and the drink seemed to have dried up the tears.

Besides, who was he, in this age of equality, to tell an adult woman she should not have another drink?

He poured her a second shot, hoping she wouldn't notice it was not quite as generous as the first one. She downed it, handed him back the empty glass and then leaned deeply back into the seat, tilted her chin up, sighed and solved the problem of distracting her by closing her eyes.

Jessica did not open her eyes for the rest of the ride, even when the driver slammed on the brakes to avoid colliding with a cab that was darting in and out of traffic and blasting his horn.

Apparently, if she'd had interest and curiosity about the sights and sounds of New York, she had totally lost that interest now. Jamie suspected any slight interest she'd had in the job was also gone, and he felt too sorry for her to even be gleeful that pushing her toward getting back on that plane was going to be so easy.

Now what? It occurred to Jamie, even to get through a few days until they got the passport sorted out, she was going to need absolutely everything, from toothpaste to a temporary phone.

He could sense the most curious feeling rising up in him. Panic?

Or maybe it was something else. That old feeling, near the surface anyway, because of the tears, coming now with a vengeance. The weight of the almost unbearable responsibility of becoming the provider for the family way too young, feeling he was totally in charge of the well-being of his mother and sister.

Once his sister was safely through college and then married, and his mother in the apartment that had been his first big purchase to celebrate his business successes, he had sworn he would never feel that way again.

Still, he was glad he had thought of it. Because little sister, Sarah, owed him a favor or two.

He had actually never thought his sister owed him anything, but desperate times called for desperate measures, as the old adage went.

He didn't realize he'd said it out loud until Jessica, without opening her eyes, said, her voice just a tiny bit slurred, "Hippocrates."

He was not sure he'd ever met a woman who could pin a quote to Hippocrates before. A woman, who by the way, was going to need everything…including underwear.

Hey, Hippocrates, can it get much more desperate than that?

Casting a glance at her, it seemed like, despite the reference to Hippocrates, she might be sleeping—or at least trying to shut out the world, not that he blamed her—he fished his phone out of his pocket and hit the message icon.

He tapped in the first letters of Sarah, and the box came up. He realized he hadn't talked to his sister since his nephew, Jared's, second birthday. A month ago. Now was not the time for guilt, however. He'd already felt guilty once today, and that was his quota for the month. Maybe the year. He didn't see any point beating around the bush, either.

Hey, I need your help.

There seemed to be quite a long pause, and then:

Who are you and what have you done with my brother?

Don't be smart. I'm serious.

What's wrong?

Just leaving JFK. I picked up a...

Jamie glanced at Jessica. Her eyes were clamped tightly shut, like a child pretending to be asleep. Some of her hair, light brown and wispy as an angel's feather, had fallen out of the clip and was lying across her cheek. But if he was not mistaken, a little purr, almost like a snore, was coming from her.

Maybe he should have given her champagne instead of cognac? This was why he needed his sister. He had a feeling, with an unknown entity like Jessica Winton, he could do everything wrong.

A business acquaintance. Her luggage was stolen. And her purse.

What? Oh, no!

She has nothing. No computer, no phone, no cash, no credit cards, no clothes.

He decided not to put the *no underwear* part. His sister was clever. She would figure it out.

What do you need from me?

He'd ignored her for a month, and yet, there she was, no questions asked, ready to do what family did. He had thought he was going to have to play his *you owe me* card but she was volunteering willingly. Really, he wasn't worthy of her, not that he planned to let that stop him from asking for her help.

But suddenly, he wasn't sure what he was asking her. He suspected it was to not let him be alone with the burden of Jessica's distress. He suspected it was to get rid of the terrible sense of failure he felt for not catching on that he was being skillfully distracted and then for not catching the thief. Now, he felt a terrible responsibility for making it all better for the small-town bookstore owner who had just experienced the very worst that New York had to offer.

That was a responsibility he could not trust himself with. At all. His sister he could trust with it.

Maybe you could take her shopping? If we could get her set up with a few basics until we figure out what to do about…

Getting rid of her seemed a touch harsh so he put:

…everything. I'll pay.

You're paying? For a shopping trip? I'm in. Is she young or old? Big or little?

Considering he was asking his sister to go shopping with a stranger, these were probably not unreasonable questions, but he felt annoyed by them. Surreptitiously, he snapped a picture of the snoozing Jessica and sent it.

The pause between texts seemed unreasonably long.

What have you done to her?

Nothing! She's had a long day. And a terrible shock. And a shot of cognac.

She's cute.

It was his turn to be silent.

In an understated way.

He remained silent.

She doesn't look like a cognac drinker.

Did that sound faintly accusatory? That was the problem with texting. The nuances of communication were completely missing. He refused to respond.

I'll get a sitter. Tomorrow morning?

Perfect.

Jamie disconnected, and thought, way too late, it might have been a mistake to involve his sister. Jessica let out a long sigh that blew a tendril of her hair up off her cheek. Her hair was coming out of the clip that held it. He had thought at first her hair was nondescript, a shade of light brown he was pretty sure they used the term "mousy" for. But there in the darkened car, only the lights from the dash and his phone screen for illumination, her hair lying across her shoulder looked as if it had been spun from unrefined gold nuggets. He was aware of that scent, subtle and sweet, a field of lavender, wrapping itself around him.

He suddenly had more misgivings about his plan. Was his sister's arrival to rescue him tomorrow enough? What about tonight? What was Jessica going to sleep in tonight? Would the hotel have a shop that was open and that sold something suitable?

He could feel a little throb beginning behind his eyes. He realized he didn't want to think about what she slept in, not tonight or any other night either.

He'd give her his credit card. She could buy

something to sleep in. He wouldn't know what it was, thank God, until the bill came. She could order food, too. It would be nice if he did that for her, but he had a feeling she was the kind of person it could prove dangerous to be nice to.

Mistake or not, he was going to be very glad to turn her over to Sarah.

CHAPTER THREE

JESSICA WOKE SLOWLY. She didn't open her eyes right away. Momentarily, she had no idea where she was. There was a lovely scent in the air—leather and spice. She wanted to just snuggle down into the deep seat, sleep, shut out the world. She was aware of noise outside, a constant hum, but in here it felt soothing and quiet.

A hand touched her shoulder, and she opened her eyes. There was a man leaning toward her. A very handsome man with gray-and-silver hair and sexy stubble and animal-dark eyes. It was his scent that was tickling her nostrils.

She smiled at him. He looked nonplussed.

And then it all came flooding back to her.

Little sleep.

No supper.

John F. Kennedy Airport.

Jamie Gilbert-Cooper.

A robbery.

Two shots of cognac.

And, added to the equation, she was pretty sure her hair was falling out of the clip she'd held it back with, and that she was sporting a pool of drool on her lovely red jacket.

Her smile faltered and then died.

The jacket that she was going to have to wear for days. Since she did not have one other thing. Not even a tissue. Oh, wait. She still had Jamie's pocket square clutched in her hand. She dabbed surreptitiously at the drool spot.

"We're at the hotel," Jamie, her potential new boss, who had now seen her bawl her eyes out, glue herself to him and pass out, told her. "We'll get you checked in, and you can do what you need to do to rest up. I'll give you my credit card so you can pick up anything you need tonight. In the morning, my sister is going to take you shopping for a few...ah, necessities."

Did the faintest wave of color move up those cheeks when he said that?

Oh, *necessities.*

Somehow it was nice, though, that he was capable of discomfort even though he looked like the kind of man who would handle a woman's *necessities* with a certain suave aplomb. It was also nice that he had a sister. A family made him a little less cover-model-for-*GQ* and a little more human.

Which was actually more dangerous than cover model!

Jessica wanted to protest the shopping trip with his sister, but really? She was not in a position to protest anything, and his sister shopping with her was a relief, given the *necessities* part of the shopping equation.

She contemplated the plight she found herself in, and the phrase *beggars cannot be choosers* took on new meaning.

Beggars, like her, who had only the clothes she wore and a borrowed pocket square. The driver held open the door of the vehicle, and the quiet of the car was invaded by the sounds of the city. Jamie exited easily, a man in his element on streets crowded with busy people, even at this time of night.

She wanted to shrink away from the sudden bustle, but Jamie was holding out a hand to her. She hesitated, then took it. His hand closed around hers, and she could feel his strength and his confidence. She also felt a little thrill of excitement that had nothing to do with her first glimpse of Manhattan.

It was in reaction to that sensation that as soon as she was free of the car, she pulled her hand out of his, unfortunately staggering a little bit when she did so. She couldn't possibly be drunk. Could she?

To her utter embarrassment, Jaime was looking at her as if he was wondering the same thing!

When was the last time she had had anything to eat? She remembered soggy eggs on toast at a hotel—that was not at all in the same league as this hotel—early this morning.

She looked past Jamie, and the streams of people enjoying a warm summer night, to the hotel. The sandstone was lit up with a floodlight and glowed like polished marble. A black awning stretched out. A uniformed doorman already held open the door in anticipation of them stepping through it.

Jessica's legs felt suddenly wobbly, and when Jamie offered his arm, she had no choice but to take it. Again, she could feel strength and confidence radiating off him.

The hotel lobby was refreshingly cool and relatively quiet after the warmth and activity outside, and it was jaw-droppingly posh. Soaring ceilings were plastered with a motif, and lit by gorgeous chandeliers, dangling crystals dancing with light. Deep rugs lay over highly polished dark hardwoods, and there was inviting furniture groupings in subtle, elegant neutrals. Under different circumstances she might appreciate it more.

Now, she wanted to say goodbye to Jamie. It would be too easy to get used to leaning on him. Jessica was not a leaner! She needed to collect herself. She wanted to go to her room and shut the door. She'd call her parents and not let on that a single thing was amiss. She'd act breezy and happy and as if she was having the adventure of her life. She'd take advantage of being in the big city and order room service. She'd have a bubble bath.

When she was feeling solid again, she would email Aubrey and Daisy. Or maybe, depending on the time differences, call one of them on WhatsApp.

They'd make her laugh about it. They'd let her know it was not the end of the world. They'd encourage her to see a fun side of it.

Then it hit her.

Email.

WhatsApp.

Part of the life of someone who owned a little something more than the rumpled clothes they wore and a damp, borrowed pocket square.

She and Jamie approached the main desk. Ever sensitive, she felt the look on the desk clerk's face seemed to change ever so slightly when he saw them. Did his nose tilt toward the air, just a tiny bit?

No luggage, she realized. And a splotch on her jacket. Her hair spilling out of the clip in an untidy mess. Her walking was just a little wobbly, despite the solid strength of the man beside her. Good grief, the desk clerk thought—

She stopped dead, and Jamie stopped beside her and looked askance at her.

"I think he thinks we're, um," she lowered her voice to a whisper, and stood on her tiptoes, "having an evening…er…tryst."

"A what?" Jamie lowered his ear to her lips.

She had a horrible temptation to nibble it. Which would confirm the clerk's worst suspicions. She wasn't drunk. She wasn't. But had the two shots been enough to lower her inhibitions? Was she looking at Jamie with the same naked avarice as Debbie had?

She could feel herself blushing thinking about

it. "We don't have any luggage. And I might look a little come-hither."

"Come-hither?"

"You know what I mean."

Clearly he did not.

"He thinks we're having a dalliance," she whispered.

Jamie reared back from her and stared at her. "Who thinks that?" he asked, a warrior look on his face like he wouldn't mind knocking some sense into someone.

She nodded toward the clerk. Jamie scowled in that direction, but didn't, apparently, reach the same conclusion as her. He looked back at her.

"Look," he said, his tone very quiet and obviously aiming for a patience and failing somewhat, "this is not the opening chapter of a Brontë novel, filled with dalliances and come-hithers and trysts."

She frowned at him, and said stiffly, "You obviously are not familiar with the opening chapters of any novel by either Charlotte or Emily."

"And thank God for that," he returned. "I'm just trying to make the point this is the big city. I'm sure in Lumber Falls people might be making note of who is checking into the local hotel with whom, but people here don't really take that kind of interest in each other."

"It's Timber Falls," she said, correcting him on the only point she could, as the other was very accurate.

He lifted a shoulder with insulting indifference to the nuances between Lumber and Timber.

And the snooty clerk was still watching them.

"He takes that kind of interest," Jessica said stubbornly.

Jamie apparently didn't care what the desk clerk thought. With a formidable expression on his face, he took her elbow, guided her up to the desk and presented a business card. She saw the attitude shift again as the clerk skimmed the card. He glanced at her again.

Like she was the main character in *Pretty Woman*. Pretransformation. Not that she looked anything like Julia Roberts.

"He's an evil little person," she said, standing on tiptoes to whisper that information into Jamie's ear. Too late, she realized to the clerk, it may have looked like a love nibble.

I am drunk, she decided. *No, not drunk. Tipsy.*

"Mr. Gilbert-Cooper, how may I assist you?"

"This is Miss Jessica Winton. You have a reservation made for her by my company?"

"I've lost my luggage," she said, as way of explanation, to erase the possible perception of a nibble of Jamie's ear and any remaining *tryst* thoughts from the clerk's mind. It occurred to her, as the clerk tapped furiously on his computer, that her breath might be boozy, and the word *lost* might have been a trifle slurred. Those facts probably overrode her explanation for her lack of luggage.

Still, how she envied him that computer! On the other hand, the hotel would have one, wouldn't they? A business center, with computers in it? Or was that old-school? Did everyone travel with their own computer now?

"Here you are," the clerk crowed, as if he was surprised to find her. "Miss Winton, if I could just have your credit card and a matching photo identification, I'll complete the booking."

"There's been an incident," she said. "I'm afraid I don't have that."

Did the clerk smirk? His every suspicion confirmed?

Jamie's tone brooked no nonsense. "The room is confirmed already on the JHA credit card. As for ID, I'll have to show you mine. Miss Winton experienced an unfortunate event at the airport. Her luggage and purse were stolen."

"I just said lost for the sake of expediency," she added. Jamie shot her a look that suggested she might not be being helpful.

"Oh," the clerk said, and his discomfort in the face of Jamie's tone seemed genuine enough, "that is very unfortunate, but I have to see the identification of everyone who stays in the hotel. It's mandatory."

"I just told you I would show you mine instead."

"Are you staying in the hotel?"

"Are you being deliberately obtuse?" Jamie asked dangerously. "She's had her identification stolen."

"Sir," the clerk's voice was actually trembling, but Jessica could not help feel he was secretly pleased by this turn of events. "I can't. Check her in. Without ID."

"My company booked the room, I'm sure you recognize the name?"

"I do, but—"

"I can give you a generous deposit against any damages."

"It's not about damages. It's a legal requirement. Homeland Security. Medical emergencies. What if, heaven forbid, the hotel caught on fire? Or what if the maid went into the room in the morning, and she was lying there, comatose?"

Was that a dig at the boozy breath? Jessica wondered, narrowing her eyes at him.

"We have to have proof on file of exactly who every person in the hotel is."

It was just like a scene from that movie. Jessica realized she, most unlikely person to ever be mistaken for a miscreant, was being refused a hotel room. The worst possible thing was happening inside of her, a slow giddy trembling. It was worse than her crying.

Jessica giggled.

Jamie and the clerk both turned to stare at her.

She put her fist to her mouth, but another giggle escaped. And then a snort of laughter. Despite her pressing against her mouth harder with her fist, more laughter.

Okay, it had a hysterical edge to it, enough so that Jamie was staring at her with concern—the *Is she going to make a scene?* kind of concern—and the clerk with an *I knew it* expression on his face.

Jamie was suddenly at her elbow, completely composed, guiding her out the door the way they had come in.

They got back in the car that had been waiting for them.

The door whispered shut and she sank into the silence, feeling as if she'd been rescued from a close call with crocodiles.

Jamie was looking straight ahead. His lips were twitching. She couldn't tell if it was with suppressed amusement or suppressed annoyance.

"I'm sorry," Jessica said. "I can't imagine what made me laugh."

"The cognac?" he suggested.

"Nerves," she insisted, trying to sound very sober. And then she added, hearing a certain defensiveness in her tone, "I haven't eaten for quite some time."

"Maybe just the absurdity of life," he suggested, rolling his shoulders back. She suspected he much preferred the burst of laughter to her earlier tears. The driver was waiting for instructions, but Jamie was obviously considering his next move.

"My place," he told the driver, finally.

Jessica felt suddenly and instantly sober. "Your place? I'm not sure. I don't think—"

"If you can think of some other options, let me know," he cut her off, his tone reflecting a souring mood. "I can drop you at the homeless shelter, if you prefer."

He groaned at the horror on her face and tilted his head back against the seat. "Sorry. Kidding."

Their choices seemed limited, indeed. But, still, his place? It seemed wildly inappropriate.

Though, just under her resistance to the idea, was a shameful curiosity. What did a man like Jamie Gilbert-Cooper live like? She was willing to bet no socks on the floor or dishes in the sink. It would be a rather intimate glimpse into his life. Under normal circumstances, she would not give in to the temptation to know a little more about him. But these were not normal circumstances.

"It will probably be just for tonight," he said. "Tomorrow, I'll have someone at the office start to figure out the details of getting your identification replaced. And getting you home."

He sounded quite eager about that, she thought.

"It's very kind of you to offer, um, your place," Jessica said. "I just don't want to put you out."

She had heard people lived small in New York City. Even very well-to-do people, which he obviously was. Was he going to sleep on the couch? Was she?

"My place is not a studio walk-up in Greenwich Village," he said, as if he could read her mind. "You won't be on a roll-out sofa for the night. I think you'll find it quite comfortable."

"Oh. It's just that—"

"You're concerned about trysts?" he asked dryly. "Dalliances?"

She blushed. "Of course not," she protested.

He, apparently, was not convinced.

"The perception of trysts? This is strictly business."

Why would she feel faintly insulted by that— as if he would never even consider a tryst with her! As if *she* needed to be reminded it was strictly business.

"I can go get a hotel if it would make you feel better," he offered. "Though I'm just not sure if it's the best idea to leave you alone. I think we should order some food as soon as we get in, since we've determined cognac is not an answer."

"Oh, I don't want you to go to any more trouble," she said, a trifle stiffly. "Just a couple of slices of toast would be fine."

"I don't cook," he said.

She cocked her head at him. *She'd been right about no dirty dishes in the sink, then.* Still, she had to ask.

"You consider toast cooking?"

"I do."

"Oh."

That should have made the differences between them more than apparent—a chasm they could not cross—but she felt, crazily, more curious about his world than ever. Perceptions of trysts aside, she realized she was *glad* she was going to his place, as if she was a science fiction fan being offered a glimpse into a world that was unimaginable until you had actually seen it with your own eyes.

"What do you think you'd like to eat?"

Toast, she thought stubbornly, but decided not to press the issue. "I bet you can get good pizza in New York City."

"I'd say the best in the world."

"My luck is changing!"

He actually smiled at her.

In that smile, she saw something you could

rely on and lean into. She had nothing. To add to her other losses today, she had just, humiliatingly, been refused a hotel room. And yet he was just the kind of man who made it seem like everything would be all right.

That *he* could make everything all right.

Tentatively, she smiled back at him. And then, before he took it as an affront to his strictly business attitude, she quickly turned her attention out her window, watching with interest as New York City unfolded before her.

He pointed it out when they passed through Times Square, and the famous Theater District. She recognized Macy's and the Metropolitan Museum of Art, the Empire State Building. The traffic was chronically snarled and it seemed to take forever to move a small distance, but the constant noise and activity outside the car held her interest. New York City was a constant swirl of movement, light and sound.

His apartment building, across from a park, impossibly seemed fancier than the hotel they had left behind. When they got out of the car, she didn't know what to look at first.

"Is that Central Park?" she asked.

He followed her gaze, and said with affection, "None other."

"I thought it would be scary. Especially at night."

Instead, she saw that even though it was now after 11:00 p.m., the park was a well-lit beautiful space. Young couples were strolling...people were walking their dogs. A runner in colorful spandex flew by. A horse-drawn carriage was clopping along in the distance.

A horse-drawn carriage ride through Central Park was on her secret list of things she wanted to do in the short period of time she was here.

"One of the many misconceptions about New York is that Central Park is not safe," Jamie told her. "The park is closed between 1:00 a.m. and 6:00 a.m. but most of the rest of the time it's pretty well populated. Naturally you would want to stay to the well-traveled paths, but it's quite beautiful at night."

In Timber Falls everything was closed after six at night! Except Wilbur's Watering Hole. Somehow, Jessica didn't want to share that with him, though.

A doorman opened the door, greeted Jamie by name and tipped his hat to her, supremely indifferent to her business with Jamie. Did that mean he came through here with women frequently, not as unfamiliar with dalliances and trysts as he was letting on?

None of your business, Jessica told herself firmly. She turned her attention to the lobby of the building, which was more understated than the hotel lobby had been, but every bit as opulent.

The lobby should have prepared her for his apartment, but it didn't. He had a special key for the elevator and it opened directly into his apartment, which made her think of something out of a James Bond movie. Lights whispered on automatically as soon as the elevator doors opened. There was a bank of floor-to-ceiling windows that looked out over the park and made the nightscape of the city that surrounded it look like a sparkling painting.

The living room, kitchen and dining room were all one large open space.

She could not stop herself from moving toward the kitchen. She ran her hand along the leathered granite of a huge kitchen island and then turned to look at the banks of white cabinets and the shining stainless steel appliances.

"It's incredible that you don't use a kitchen that looks like this," she mused. "Look at it. Double ovens!"

"What does one use a double oven for?"

She shot him a look to see if he was kidding. He was not.

"Thanksgiving dinner. Christmas dinner." She could not contain a sigh of pure longing. "Turkey in one. Pies in the other. It's always a problem."

He was giving her a look as if she came from another planet. That look should have been enough to stop her exploring, but no, she might never see anything like this again.

She shamelessly oohed and ahhed over the wine cooler, a built-in barista-style coffee maker, the cleverly hidden pull-out-drawer-style dishwasher.

She stopped at the fridge. "It looks big enough to park a Volkswagen in," she said. "Can I peek inside?"

He nodded, watching her with *that* look, the one she couldn't quite decipher. The one where she didn't know if he found her annoying or amusing.

The fridge had zones in it! And yet, it was relatively empty. A few condiments, a container of cream, three bottles of imported beer.

The fridge seemed to mirror the rest of his space. Nothing had a "used" look to it. The polished counters were bare of the clutter of daily life. There wasn't even a sugar bowl or a paper roll out. Where were the dish towels?

She turned her attention to the rest of the space. No books out, not even a newspaper tossed carelessly. No family pictures. Definitely no socks. The artwork was gorgeous, but all abstract, revealing nothing about him.

The space should have cemented him in her mind as what he was: cosmopolitan, busy, not home much.

Instead, the perfection of it, the ready-for-the-posh-interiors-magazine-cover-shoot, made her feel oddly sad. His home was beautiful, and yet it did not have any soul.

When she turned to study him, it was obvious to her that he was beautiful, too, but that he did have soul, a great strength of character, a composure that rose above the inevitable chaos of life.

"Your space is gorgeous," she said, quietly.

"Why do I sense a *but*?" he asked, cocking his head at her.

"It doesn't really suit you," she ventured, feeling as if she was being way too personal, and at the same time that honesty was called for.

"Ah. I'll have to speak to the designer about that." She could tell he wanted to leave it there, but curiosity got the better of him. "In what way doesn't it suit me?"

She did not know him well enough to weigh in on that. He could be her future boss, after all. Still, she couldn't stop herself.

"It doesn't feel like a home. It feels like a hotel."

For a moment, he looked stunned. And then he raised an eyebrow at her. "But that suits me perfectly," he said.

No, it doesn't. For just a moment, she could picture him tossing a child in the air, toys on the floor, the space filled with the good smells of things cooking and laughter and motion, and his vitality.

That imagined picture brought a tinge of color to her cheeks.

It had just been a too long and eventful day that had brought on this flight of fancy. You did not picture the man who could be your boss— obviously single and successful and not willing to change one thing about his glorious playboy lifestyle—in a scene of domestic contentment.

Was she in that scene with him? Good grief! Was that *their* baby the Jamie of her imagination was playing with?

The renegade thoughts were stunning. She had put away such longings what seemed to be a lifetime ago. To hope for such things was to reopen a place in herself that was completely barricaded from the possibility of ever hurting the way she had once hurt...hadn't she known, even when she met Ralph in Copenhagen, he could not touch that place inside of her? But this man...

"I have to call my parents," she blurted out, as a way of grounding herself.

"Sure. Let's just get the pizza ordered first. Have a seat," he invited with a careless sweep of his hand. He was unknotting the tie from his throat, and it felt enticingly intimate to witness that moment. She scurried over to a deep leather chair that looked toward the view, instead of at him.

"Pizza," he said, still taking charge, still solving problems. Of which, she reminded herself firmly, she was one. "Any preferences?"

"The wilder the better," she said.

When she cast a look at him, she could see his mouth had dropped open, and she was happy to have surprised him.

He was studying her with interest. "You are a walking contradiction, aren't you? The big family gathering dinners, and then the wilder the better taste."

Her happiness at his surprise dissolved as she realized the possibility for double entendre. "I was only talking about pizza!" she stammered.

"Of course you were," he said soothingly, but not before she saw the wicked satisfaction cross his features. She had caught him off balance by weighing in on his style, and now he was enjoying catching her off balance, as well.

"Don't you have traditional family celebrations here?" she asked him, remembering he had mentioned his sister, the one who would be shopping with her tomorrow.

"No," he said, a little too curtly, as if by asking about his family, she had crossed a line.

"I have to call my parents," she reminded him—and herself—again. And she could see the fact she was going to check in with her parents negated, completely, any wild thoughts he was having concerning her.

As if.

He ordered pizza first. When he handed her the phone, she said, "Please keep track of the costs, for the pizza and the long-distance call. I'll pay my share when I have funds."

His lips twitched. Again, she could not tell if it was amusement or annoyance. He didn't address her offer to pay at all, just handed her the phone.

"Let me show you the guest room and you can make your call there in privacy—"

As if she would have anything *private* to say to her parents.

Hey, Mom…hey, Dad. It's been a crazy introduction to New York City. I've been robbed, but rescued by this gorgeous man who might be my boss someday if I abandon you and Timber Falls, and by the way I'm staying in his apartment with him.

Her mom would have a heart attack and her dad would be on the next plane to New York.

"—and freshen up. By the time you're done, the pizza should have arrived."

Jessica trailed him down a wide hallway, taking a peek in the master bedroom as they went by. It faced those same Central Park city views, and held a massive bed that made her think, to her eternal horror, *the wilder the better.*

The guest room was gorgeous. The views did not face the park, and yet the cityscape was utterly breathtaking. He showed her through to the attached bath, and she saw it had a stand-alone tub and a deluxe Italian-tiled shower stall in it.

Bubble bath? Or shower? Somehow, she was not sure she could stand having a bubble bath in the same space he was in, even if walls did separate them. Besides, she was hungry, and a proper bath required a commitment of time.

Shower it would be, and she could not wait!

"Do you suppose I could borrow a T-shirt to use as a nightie?"

"Of course," he said smoothly, but something had flashed, just for a moment in the dark depths of those eyes, when she mentioned a nightie.

Or maybe not, because he continued speaking, the ideal host, unruffled by mentions of nighties. "Meanwhile, there's a canvas bag on the back of your bathroom door, if you put your clothes in that and set it outside, I'll have the concierge pick them up and have it laundered."

"At this time of night?"

He lifted his shoulder. Obviously anything was possible here, at any time of the night or day, and he didn't give it a second thought.

"So, you don't cook *or* do laundry?" she asked. The truth was that the thought of someone else doing her laundry was embarrassing to her.

"I'm often short on time. I cheerfully delegate anything I don't enjoy doing."

He left her, and then came back a few minutes later, knocking softly on her door before coming in and placing a selection of neatly folded T-shirts on her bed. Then he laid a plaid bathrobe—obviously his—beside the shirts.

He gave her his security code and left her his phone, then closed the doors behind him. Jessica unlocked the phone and called her parents. How high school crush was it that she was aware that her mouth on the phone was very close to where Jamie's mouth had been on that same phone?

I do not have any kind of crush on Jamie Gilbert-Cooper, Jessica told herself sternly.

He was her rescuer in a bad situation. Naturally, there would be some feelings of transference, like a hostage might feel for the Navy SEAL who saved her from a certain and horrible death at the hands of bad guys.

When her father picked up the phone, he wanted to know, immediately, why she was calling from a strange number. Her mother had started to worry an hour ago, and had been texting her. They were on speakerphone now, her mother denying she had been worried.

"I seem to be having trouble with the international phone plan I ordered," Jessica said. "It might be better if you didn't text me for a bit. I think I have to pay per text, and I'm not getting them anyway."

She hated lying to her parents, but she hated the thought of them worrying even more. She told them, breezily, she had been dropped into an episode of *Lifestyles of the Rich and Famous.* Without mentioning she was in a private apartment, she described the room she was in to her home decorating channel obsessed mother.

"Send me a picture," her mother said. "Or put some on Facebook."

"Um, I will when I get my phone plan sorted out. I don't want to use any data just yet."

"Doesn't the hotel have internet?" her mother insisted.

"Oh, it's late here. I'll try to do some Facebook updates tomorrow." From the computer at the public library. That was on her list of must-sees. The New York Public Library. "I haven't eaten yet."

"Don't go out by yourself!" her mother warned.

"Don't worry, I'm ordering pizza."

After listening to a long list of instructions from her mother about opening her hotel door to the deliveryman, she tried to hang up. But her mother had to give her quite a lengthy description of her father fiddling with a lock system for the house and her store that could be operated from a cell phone. Jessica was finally able to disengage. She wondered about her impatience. Was it because Jamie would be waiting for her with pizza? She couldn't help but also wonder what he would make of an adult woman getting those kind of instructions from her mother.

Maybe Daisy and Aubrey were right when they weighed in that perhaps her life was too small.

Suffocating.

The word, popping into her head, stunned Jessica, and made her feel guilty. She quickly turned her thoughts in a different direction.

She had his cell phone. She had his security code. She could sign in and send a quick private message to her friends. Or she could have a quick look through his photos. It would tell her all kinds of delicious information about her host.

She was not that kind of person! Snoopy and deceitful.

One little look...

No! Before she could change her mind she took his phone back out to him. He pocketed it with a quick nod, as if it had never even occurred to him that she might have a peek at the information on it.

Did that make her trustworthy? Or just plain boring?

She retreated back to her room and to the bathroom. She stripped off her travel-rumpled clothes, and the water from the shower pounding down did literally wash away all her cares. Jessica was not sure a shower had ever felt quite as wonderful as this one. The hot water alternated, blissfully, between pounding, spraying and misting. She accidentally touched a button and was bathed in soothing light. And then, more purposefully, she touched another button. Music flooded the shower stall.

Coincidentally, it was Daisy's first number one hit single, "Nothing is Impossible."

As the water massaged her skin, and the music

spoke to her as if Daisy was right here coaxing her to dream big, Jessica was aware of feeling not frightened and not put out, but finally, relaxed and safe.

But it was more than that. And it was more than the contortions of the water coming from that showerhead that were making her skin tingle.

She became aware she felt fully and completely alive.

The sensation increased as she stepped out of the shower and toweled off with deeply luxurious pure white Egyptian cotton towels, and then padded out to the bedroom and chose one of Jamie's T-shirts to slip over her head.

Despite the crispness of it, it smelled of him: clean and spicy, fragrant in an exquisitely masculine way that made all her senses vibrate, as if the air itself had taken on a quality that stroked her.

Feeling life so intensely begged the question: How did she feel most of the time? Asleep? Operating on some kind of autopilot?

Was it a reaction to overcoming a crisis that was bringing her this sense of being exquisitely and intensely aware of everything? Absolutely every single thing that could have gone wrong had, and yet, here she stood, more than a survivor, life handing her completely unexpected gifts.

Or was it from being in Jamie Gilbert-Cooper's space, surrounded by his things and his scents, his powerful energy permeating the very air she was breathing that left her feeling so aware? Perhaps when you had his kind of energy, you didn't have to decorate a space to reflect who you were?

She had a thought even more troubling. Was this sensation of being so alive, so open to what happened next, so ready for the strange adventure she found herself in, a message from her life?

Aubrey and Daisy had been hinting almost from the beginning that Jessica was in a rut, was playing it too safe, was not open to the truly sensational experience that was life.

It was true. Since her fiancé, Devon, had died what she had wanted, more than any other single thing, was for life to feel safe again. But in this moment, she was aware she didn't want that at all.

Jessica felt suddenly powerful, as if, just as

Daisy's music had suggested, nothing was impossible. As if she could change her whole life and her whole outlook right now, right this very second.

For the first time it occurred to her that maybe she was going to accept this job offer.

And then, she eyed the bathrobe he had brought in. It was a man's, huge and plaid, and way too bulky for a summer night.

She shoved all her dirty laundry into the bag Jamie had provided. Let someone else do her laundry! The new Jessica Winton—bold, embracing the adventure of life—threw open her bedroom door and walked out into that luxe apartment in nothing more than her future boss's oversize T-shirt.

Well, she might have been hiding behind the laundry bag, just a touch.

CHAPTER FOUR

WHILE JESSICA WAS in the shower, Jamie waited for pizza—the-wilder-the-better-be-careful-what-you-ask-for-sweetheart-pizza—to be delivered.

Pizza. She was in New York City. She could have had anything. He had a list of favorite high-end five-star restaurants that were happy to deliver. But no, she wanted pizza, and insisted that she would pay her half when she had some funds.

Who walked into an apartment like this one—at one of New York's toniest addresses, the three-block stretch that formed Central Park South—and demanded to pay for half the pizza?

The same woman who had seen something here—or a lack of something—that no one else had ever seen. Seen something about *him* that people did not see.

The same woman who looked at his quarter-million-dollar kitchen remodel and did not see *arrival* but wondered about Christmas dinner. He had a feeling that she would not approve of the fact there had never even been a Christmas dinner here. There had never even been a Christmas tree.

She wouldn't approve, either, that the last female guest to his apartment had not had turkey on her mind. In fact, she'd had quite an interesting idea of what the kitchen island could be used for.

He had sent her home without testing her idea. He realized, now, something he had not realized at the time. It was probably the influence of his guest that made him articulate, within his own mind, what he had felt when his last disappointed guest had left the apartment.

Jamie was sick of the kind of women he had deliberately populated his life with. Fast and sophisticated, they liked all the trappings of success that this apartment represented. They didn't complicate his life.

Not a single one of them had ever suggested, of his space, *it doesn't really suit you.*

Why did he care about Jessica Winton's approval? *I do not* he told himself, but he was aware it was not quite the truth.

That very same woman who was worried a hotel desk clerk thought she was sporting a come-hither look was the kind of woman who could complicate a man's life before he knew what had hit him.

Jamie decided to entertain himself by looking up the phrase *come-hither*. It turned out the saying dated back to the 1800s. It indicated a look of sexual invitation, flirtation and seduction.

Even though he could not think of one person less likely than her to have such a look, he put down his phone as if it had burned him.

Who used a phrase like that?

A bookstore owner, apparently. One who also was familiar with quotes from Hippocrates and the works of the Brontë sisters.

Down the hall, he could hear the shower running in the spare bedroom en suite bathroom. She—Jessica Winton, of come-hither fame— was in his space.

But there would be no come-hithering of any sort. He was a professional. She was a professional. They had been dealt an unexpected hand. They would deal with it professionally. He heard the shower turn off. He imagined her dressed in nothing but a cloud of steam.

She had borrowed his phone to call her parents, he reminded himself. Not one single woman who moved in his circles called her parents to check in. Not under any circumstances.

She wouldn't be calling her parents if she had a boyfriend, or significant other. She'd be calling him. She wouldn't have come to New York to investigate a job opportunity, either.

Why was his brain insisting on acting like it had uncovered a very important truth about her? That she was single?

All he needed to know about Jessica Winton was that she was wholesome and innocent and in need of protection. And professionalism. Until he got rid of her. He was probably going to be struck dead with a bolt of lightning for even thinking of her dressed in only a cloud of steam.

When the doorman rang to let him know the pizza was here, Jamie nearly jumped out of his skin. He hated it that his unexpected charge had him wound up tight in some way he was not accustomed to. He elected to go down to the lobby and get the pizza, rather than have it brought up. He took the stairs.

When he came back into the living room, puffing slightly, Jessica was standing at the floor-to-ceiling window, in one of his T-shirts.

The value of the take-his-mind-off-Jessica run down the stairs was instantly dissolved. He might as well have saved his energy.

The T-shirt was falling off one of her shoulders, leaving it completely bare. The shoulder seams came down to her elbows, and the hem of the shirt ended past her knees. She didn't have on a speck of makeup or a piece of jewelry.

She hadn't put on the bathrobe he had provided, and though that was completely understandable—it would have been way too large for her and it was summertime, not winter—he resented it.

Because there was something about her standing there, in only a T-shirt, her legs long and bare and slender, her body faintly and femininely curved against the thin fabric, that made his mouth go dry.

Jamie chided himself that he saw much more provocative outfits in the office daily. Really, she should have looked like a child playing dress-up.

Jessica turned and looked at him. Her hair was wet and curling, her face flushed pink from the shower. Her eyes looked huge, as seductive as the chocolate that they matched. She did not look like any kind of child at all. She did not look like she was innocent or in need of protection, either.

Her expression was about the furthest thing from come-hither that he could ever imagine. And yet he was unbelievably aware of her.

"The view is amazing."

He thought it was, too, and he didn't mean the park.

"Thanks," he said, congratulating himself on his professional tone, "I like it."

"I had no idea that Central Park was so huge," she said turning back to the window.

"It's eight hundred and forty acres. Forty-two million people a year visit it." He congratulated himself on the utter safety of a tour-guide-to-client conversation.

Forty million, nine hundred and ninety-nine thousand and ninety-nine of whom, had they seen his apartment, would have just taken it at face value. They would have seen arrival and success. Not a vague emptiness.

But she hadn't used the word *empty*. So where had that come from, that indictment of his life?

He glanced at his dining room table. Would he

sit next to her? Across from her? Which would be less dangerous?

"It's a nice night," he said. "Do you want to eat pizza alfresco?" Side by side, on his deck, an end table in between them, less chance of those naked little toes touching him, or shoulders brushing, or eyes meeting. They could look at the view, instead of each other.

She laughed and he raised an eyebrow at her.

"In Italian," she explained, "that phrase means 'in the cool.' Usually, when an Italian says it, it refers to spending time in jail."

"You speak Italian?" he asked, incredulous. He had a sudden, totally unwanted vision, of her leaning in to him whispering, *Voglio fare l'amore con te.*

As if Jessica Winton would ever say something like that! It was wrong to even think it. It was right up there with come-hithering. Thankfully, she did not speak Italian.

"I just seem to collect information," she told him.

"Dibs on you for my Trivial Pursuit team." The weird thing was, he could picture playing Trivial Pursuit with her. At the Christmas celebration he had never hosted. Jamie gave his head a shake in an effort to clear any vision of Jessica Winton inhabiting any part of his future.

Not Christmas dinner. Not sexy Italian phrases. Not playing a game at the annual office party. Not come-hithering.

He slid the patio door open and the sounds of the city, along with warm summer air, rushed in. He held the door back, balancing the pizza in his hand, letting her go out first.

As she brushed by him, the lavender smell—the one that invoked visions of her, and possibly him, in a purple field together—was, thankfully, completely gone.

It was, unfortunately, replaced with something even more tantalizing.

Soap. Skin. Squeaky-clean hair. Something so purely feminine, it took his breath away.

He held the pizza box closer to his nose, hoping to banish all else. He pulled out a chair for her with his toe, and then set the pizza box on the table and took a chair on the opposite side of it. The park was growing quiet—it was probably close to midnight.

"Look! There's still a horse and carriage."

"I think they book the last rides at eleven thirty."

She got up from the table, and went to the railing. "It's a young couple," she reported. "Oh, my gosh, I think he's asking her to marry him. Come see."

Though it was against his better judgment, he joined her at the railing. Sure enough, eleven stories below them, a young man was presenting what looked to be a ring box to a young woman. Her squeal of delight rose over every other sound in the night.

"It's like something out of a fairy tale," Jessica said, with a happy sigh. As she turned back to the table, her shoulder—the naked one—brushed his arm.

Cue the music, he thought, to banish any red-hot thoughts that accidental brush, the one he had been hoping to avoid by choosing to dine alfresco, might cause. *Someday, my prince will come*. That was it *exactly*. Jessica Winton had the starstuck look on her face of a woman in search of a prince.

Scary.

Even scarier was his curiosity about why she hadn't found one.

He opened the pizza box, and offered her

a slice. She took one, took a delicate bite and closed her eyes.

"Wild enough for you?" he asked.

She opened her eyes and glanced at him. He kept his expression deliberately bland. *Professional*, he congratulated himself.

"Definitely wild. And delicious. I come from a pepperoni-only family and I always seem to cave to the majority. This is a treat. Some kind of Mediterranean, right? Olives? Onions? Feta cheese?"

"Plus anchovies and hot pickles. Here. I'll show you how to eat it like a New Yorker."

"New Yorkers eat pizza a certain way?"

"Of course." As she watched, he took the crust and rolled it neatly toward the triangular tip of the pizza.

"But now it's a sausage roll, not pizza!" she protested, watching him.

He took a bite, aware of her eyes on his lips, before they skittered away. "Try it before you knock it."

And so she did. She closed her eyes with pleasure as she bit into it. Now his eyes were on her lips!

"And so practical, too," she decided.

Considering how aware they both seemed to be now of each other's lips, he wasn't so sure about that.

"So," he said, after they had both staved off the worst of the hunger and were working on their second slices, "tell me why you think you might like to work for JHA. Because you don't really seem like the type who ends up in marketing."

Terrible timing for a job interview.

And yet he could not think of a better way to get his mind off the lusciousness of her lips closing over that roll of pizza. When he dragged his eyes from her lips, he noticed her naked leg sticking out from under his T-shirt. Her toenails were painted the palest shade of pink.

"The type?" she said. "What type do I seem like?"

The type who was targeted by thieves looking for an innocent. The type who phoned her parents. The type who harbored a belief—however secret—in fairy tales.

"I guess you don't seem like the type who would leave everything you know behind to find a new life," he said carefully.

"Really?" she said, the deliberately light tone of someone who was hiding something, "This pizza alone is enough to make me toss my old life."

"Pizza preferences aside, you seem like a picket fences kind of woman. And a solid guy who adores you and whose world revolves around you. Babies. A golden retriever. A summer cottage on the lake. A big Christmas tree, only real will do."

He was pretty sure, according to the employment standard act, you weren't allowed to say anything like that to a prospective employee. It was probably sexist as all get-out to offer conjecture about her lifestyle but he was deliberately trying to provoke her.

"Are you reaching these conclusions because I think your oven is ideally suited to the preparation of traditional feasts?" she asked. "Or because I think your house is more like a hotel than a home?"

"Traditional," he said. "That's what I'm trying to say. You seem more traditional than career oriented."

"And yet," she said calmly, "I've enjoyed great success in my career. I assume that's part of why I was invited here."

Sitting here on his deck, the sounds of New

York calming for the night, the warm summer air embracing them, it felt as if he needed to know *more* about her than the career synopsis that had been put together for him by an office assistant. Admittedly, he had not even glanced at it until he got to JFK to pick her up.

"Though I did grow up with very traditional values and a lifestyle very close to what you described," she said, after a moment. "It's the life my parents had, and the life I always thought I would have, too."

"What made you change your mind?"

She hesitated. "That solid guy who adored me died."

"I'm so sorry." He looked at her face. He hadn't turned on the patio light, and it was alabaster in the subdued secondary lights from the city and the other apartments. Really, his intent had been a kind of casual job interview, not a prying into her personal life. But suddenly, he *had* to know. "Will you tell me what happened?"

"The world I grew up in, and that I always wanted—safe, predictable, traditional—was shattered in a second. Devon died in a skiing accident." Softly she said, "I don't want to leave myself open to believing in happily-ever-after again."

But he had the feeling she did, she just didn't want to believe she did.

"Tell me about the two of you."

Really?

Good night, Miss Winton, nice to make your acquaintance would have been the wiser choice!

Jamie did not have these kinds of conversations with people. And especially not female people who might be working for him someday soon.

"We grew up together," Jessica said. "I started preschool the same day Devon did. We had the same friends. Our parents were friends. We lived down the block from each other. We enjoyed all the things that growing up in a place like Timber Falls had to offer—hiking and camping, skiing and snowshoeing.

"We never really *fell* in love. We were always in love. We always knew, both of us, that we had been together forever and we always would be. But then, we weren't. He died our senior year in high school."

"He asked you to marry him in high school?" He couldn't keep the shock out of his voice.

She nodded, and tilted her chin at him, with faint stubbornness that said, *Just because we were young doesn't mean it wasn't real.*

Jamie grappled with what he was hearing. He knew from the fact sheet he had been given about her that she was twenty-six years old. That meant high school was seven or eight years behind her. It troubled him that even before high school she had been making huge choices. It sounded awfully young to be mapping out the entire course of your life, and choosing a life partner. It seemed criminal, somehow, that she had missed out on the experience of falling in love.

Not that he was one to talk about that! He'd avoided the complications of falling in love like it was a plague.

So, instead of saying any of that to her—that she had been too young, that she had missed something—he was shocked to hear himself saying, "I was only eighteen when my dad died, so I know how tragedy shapes a person."

She cocked her head at him. A man could fall toward what he saw in her eyes: someone who *knew* what it was to have your heart break in so many pieces it could not possibly be put back together again.

It felt imperative he get this back on track—that he not fall toward the respite offered by her eyes—so he carefully rephrased his original question. "So what makes a woman like you leave everything she knows in search of a new start?"

"I do have a really good life in Timber Falls," Jessica said hastily. "I have my bookstore and my family..." Her voice trailed away.

"But?" he asked her.

"You're probably absolutely right. I don't think of myself as the marketing type, but there must be a reason I came to JHA's attention. I made it clear that I'm not at all sure about this position, but I love bookstores, I love books, I love authors and I love readers. I've come up with an equation for putting all those elements together success-fully. I can't take it any further in Timber Falls and sometimes I feel a longing for *more*, even though I don't know what that *more* is."

She had thrown that *love* word around pretty casually, but what if that was what she was re-ally longing for? What if that was her *more*? The one she wasn't admitting, even to herself.

Jamie could feel a longing, unknown to him before this very second, rise up in his own soul.

"A couple of years ago, I met a guy online," she admitted, embarrassed. "He was from Europe. We met for the first time in Copenhagen. It was a disaster."

She was telling him it wasn't *love* she was after, after all. It should have been a relief to hear it, and yet…

"So when the invitation from JHA came, 95 percent of me said *don't be ridiculous* and 5 percent said *just go see.* And here I am." She smiled at him. "Seeing."

In the darkness her eyes seemed luminous, and her lips lush. He could smell the scent of her above the scent of the pizza.

It felt as if he was seeing something, too.

He had every trapping of success, and yet she was making him aware, again, of some dangerous emptiness. There was something about her that was fresh and tantalizing and as foreign to his world as all this was to hers. He felt a pull to see where the merging of their two worlds could lead. It felt utterly dangerous.

And irresponsible, as well.

It must just be the lateness of the hour making him think these uncharacteristic thoughts. The lateness of the hour, the oddness of having a stranger in his space, in his T-shirt, munching pizza with a most delectable mouth.

He glanced at his phone. "It's gotten very late," he said. "Would you be more comfortable if I got a hotel for the night?"

"No, of course not!"

He considered the possibility that *he* might be more comfortable, and then dismissed it. He found her refreshing and attractive. Disgracefully, there was something he wanted to challenge about her belief in that teenage love. One taste of adult passion—the wilder, the better— could break her out of that almost childish loyalty to old memories.

Jamie drew himself up short. He could handle her under the same roof for one night. He was not a Neanderthal, not a *me Tarzan, you Jane* kind of guy, at all. And there was nothing he could teach anyone about the complexity of human relationships.

"I had some things arranged for you for tomorrow, but I'm going to have to rearrange them," he told her, all professional, again. "Getting you a few necessities and getting your paperwork in order seems like it should be a priority. I'll look after it first thing in the morning."

"Thank you," she said.

There, he congratulated himself, very businesslike, indeed.

The moment of temptation had passed, and he would hand her off to his sister and other assistants so that another moment of temptation did not rise up to take its place.

"Good night, then," he said, got up and quickly went back inside. He dispensed her laundry to the lobby with an urgent tag on it, and had just gotten in his bedroom and closed the door when his phone lit up, an incoming text from Sarah.

Sorry, it's late.

It's okay. I'm up.

Jared's sick. He was at a birthday party. I think he might have overdone the cake and ice cream. All the evidence points in that direction.

If he encouraged her, he was going to get a picture of the evidence, so he typed in:

Spare me the details.

Not going to be able to make the shopping trip tomorrow. Take her to Hennessey's on Fifth. Ask for Meredith.

He contemplated that. He'd been planning on turning Jessica over. Getting away from her.

How is she holding up?

Fine.

And then, before his sister could ferret out the fact Jessica was staying here, in the same apartment as him, Jamie quickly typed in that he was sure Jared would be okay.

You always promise that.

He stared at the phone, thinking how odd it was she would say that when he had thought of it today for the first time in a long time.

And you're almost always right.

That part surprised him. Had those paltry words he had offered his family really brought anyone any comfort? He focused on the *almost*.

It was a good reminder, in the emotional support department, he had nothing to offer.

A case in point: thinking that kissing a young woman, who still held a torch for a long dead young man, could somehow bring her back to life, like a princess who slept.

Jamie shook his head. Fairy tales, now? It wasn't the Brontë sisters, but it was evidence that the small-town bookstore owner who had invaded his apartment really was a bad influence on him.

He contemplated the unfortunate turn of his life: he was going shopping at Hennessey's. No, he wasn't. He was turning Jessica over to some capable shopping person named Meredith, presumably an expert. Then he was walking to his office, which was just off Fifth, and he was assigning one of his assistants all things Jessica-related: police report, passport replacement, a little New York sightseeing, meetings with a few selected clients. He would make sure it was on the assignment list that as soon as she had replaced her ID, they would get her into her own hotel room.

But at the same time Jamie was making plans to distance himself from his guest, he was aware of a little voice in the back of his mind, warning him: from the first moment he had laid eyes on Jessica Winton not one single thing had gone according to his plan.

CHAPTER FIVE

JESSICA SAT OUT on the deck for a while longer, drinking in the sumptuousness of the night. She wasn't quite sure what had just happened. Jamie's departure had seemed abrupt.

Had she said or done something? She shouldn't have told him so much about Devon, about her personal life. It was the long and eventful day that had encouraged uncharacteristic confidences from her.

And yet even with Devon freshly in her mind, she could not help but wonder if Jamie was just as aware as she herself was, that as unlikely as it seemed, there was a chemistry between them.

After a long time of thinking about that, she got up and went to bed. She was still on Canadian time, and it wasn't that late in British Columbia. There was a television in the room, but she felt no desire to turn it on.

Oddly, she was not missing her internet connection, either.

She felt no need at all to report on the circumstances she found herself in, but rather she wanted to keep them to herself, as if they were a secret she was nurturing. There was something freeing about just allowing herself to have an experience, instead of feeling a need to divulge it to her online world.

She slid between luxurious sheets and snuggled under the lightweight down comforter. It occurred to her she should be worried: she was no closer to having cash, replacing her credit cards or getting a passport so that she could travel home at the scheduled time.

Oddly enough, when she closed her eyes, she realized she had rarely felt less worried in her entire life.

How much did that have to do with Jamie Gilbert-Cooper taking charge? She was asleep before she could answer the question.

Jessica awoke in the morning to a soft rap on her door. When she opened it, there was no one there, but the laundry bag was outside and her jacket, enclosed in a thick paper wrap, was on a hangar that had been put on the doorknob. There was also a small bag of toiletries: toothbrush, toothpaste, deodorant.

For one mortifying minute she considered that he was trying to tell her something, but then she realized that was the *old* Jessica, too sensitive and too serious. Of course he wasn't trying to tell her something—like that her breath was bad, though after the pizza last night that did seem like a possibility—he was being considerate!

Brushing her teeth felt exquisite. But when she pulled her hair back into its clip, put her freshly laundered clothes on, and looked at herself in the full-length mirror behind the bathroom door, she came face-to-face with that *old* Jessica.

How could she have changed so much in less than twenty-four hours? She *hated* the outfit. It seemed dull and conservative, appropriate for the floor of the Canadian House of Commons, perhaps, but for a few days in New York City? Not so much.

When she went shopping with Jamie's sister today, she was going to choose items that were appropriate business attire, but not quite so staid. But she still had to be practical. She still had to choose things she could wear in Timber Falls.

Could you choose clothes that were practical

and sexy? It was a dilemma she had not found herself in before, not even when she was shopping for her trip to Copenhagen. Shouldn't she have known something was off with her first face-to-face meeting with Ralph when, instead of thinking of items that would be attractive, she had been thinking of travel practicalities, like wrinkle-free?

She realized she was looking forward to meeting Jamie's sister. She wasn't going to pry, but she was sure his sister would drop all kinds of clues as to who Jamie really was that his apartment was not giving away.

Jessica also hoped Jamie's sister was good at fashion. She herself sucked at it. There was nothing about the growing up in Timber Falls experience that encouraged fashion-forward thinking. It was an outdoorsy lifestyle that lent itself to plaid shirts and khaki shorts and sturdy shoes for both genders. Business attire at the bookstore was blue jeans and a blouse in the summer, blue jeans and a sweater in the winter.

Jessica had a book-themed sweater collection that children adored. She felt embarrassed just thinking about it! There would be no sweaters with embroidered cats on them today. No, it was summer and she was in New York. She wanted her style to reflect something a little bolder.

Fashion-wise, would she recognize those things? She didn't want to go over the top, after all. Once again, she longed for her phone. With it, she could have consulted with Aubrey and Daisy right from the change room, time differences notwithstanding. She could have snapped selfies and sent them, a virtual fashion show and consultation.

She stepped out of her bedroom. At the last moment, she pulled the clip from her hair, and ran a hasty hand through it.

The apartment was flooded with light. The kitchen island had on it a selection of pastries, croissants, bagels, breads and spreads.

"Good morning." He looked at her only briefly. Did his eyes rest, for a moment, on her loose hair, before he looked hastily away?

Jamie Gilbert-Cooper was standing there, sipping coffee from a take-out cup and leafing through a newspaper he had on the counter in front of him.

She used his concentration on the paper to quickly study him. Yup. Her first impression of him was confirmed: gorgeous. He had obviously already showered: his silver hair was damp and impossibly shiny, his skin had that tender, touchable look of being freshly shaved.

He was dressed, more casually than yesterday, but still in the kind of clothes that in Timber Falls would have been reserved for a wedding. Or a funeral.

Which suddenly struck her as faintly pathetic, though she felt instantly disloyal to her hometown.

He was wearing a white shirt, with a subtle pattern in it. It was opened at the throat and rolled at the cuffs. It was tucked underneath a belt that was threaded through the loops of gray, knife-pressed pants. He had on loafers, with no socks. In Timber Falls no one ever wore shoes in the house.

"This one's for you," he said, pointing at a coffee. "I didn't put anything in it, but I brought creamers and sugar packs."

"You have a coffee maker like that—" she gestured to the machine built into his cabinetry "—and you pick it up?"

He glanced at the coffee maker. "I'm not sure I've ever used that. I pick up coffee and breakfast on the way to work. There's the best little shop just down the street. Taste it and tell me if you think I could do as well."

She picked up her coffee, removed the lid and added some cream to it. The aroma was heady, and she took a sip.

"That's not coffee," she said. "That's ambrosia."

He smiled. "Welcome to New York City. A better welcome than yesterday."

She decided she had not experienced too many things as dangerous as Jamie Gilbert-Cooper smiling at her as she drank the best coffee she had ever had. After a minute, she chose a croissant. It was so flaky, light and buttery, she thought she was going to die. Sensory overload!

"I had a quick look online this morning," he told her. "You must have travel insurance, right?"

"Yes, I do."

"I'm sure they'll cover your losses. We'll need to file the police report in order for you to make a claim, though."

Her mouth fell open. "I hadn't even thought of that."

"Have some breakfast, and then give them a call."

"Thank you, I will." She hoped it wasn't a

weakness to feel so good about having someone to lean on, someone to take charge, to help her navigate all the messy details of putting her life back together.

And it wasn't just the current messiness. After Devon, she had never really put her life back together. Maybe, just maybe, this was her chance. Maybe this was why she had been drawn to New York as if tugged by an invisible thread.

"Which do you want to do first?" Jamie asked. "Canadian consular services, or shopping?"

"What's more convenient for your sister? What's her name, by the way?"

"Sarah." He looked uncomfortable. "My nephew was sick last night. I think she's going to bow out."

"How old is your nephew? Is he okay?"

"Jared is two, apparently suffering from a birthday cake overdose, the little oinker."

She heard the affection in his voice, and again, could imagine him throwing a laughing child in the air.

As sorry as she was for the missed opportunity to ferret out the family perspective on Jamie, and as sorry as she was that his nephew was sick, she felt the tiniest little tickle of pure anticipation.

"Let's go shopping first," she decided, aching to get rid of the clothes she was wearing the way she assumed a snake must ache to get rid of its old skin.

"Shopping it is," he said with so little enthusiasm she burst out laughing.

And then he was laughing, too.

And it felt, oddly and beautifully, like one of the most glorious moments of her entire life.

Which, she told herself sternly, just meant everyone was right. She had been far too sheltered. She had lived way too small. She had used a dreadful event to cling to safety, as if the whole world was a life raft that could capsize at any time.

Jamie was a charming man, used to these kinds of intimate little interchanges with the opposite sex.

She needed to be very wary of being enchanted by him.

But the new her insisted on poo-poohing her wariness. It wasn't as if they had posted banns for marriage. They were going shopping. She needed to loosen up and learn to have fun.

A sensation of freedom overcame her. Not a

single person here knew her. There was a lovely anonymity to being here.

Not like Timber Falls, which was akin to living in the proverbial goldfish bowl.

Suffocating, a small inner voice offered helpfully.

For the second time.

She shrugged it off, finished her coffee and her croissant, and felt ready, not for a shopping trip, but for the adventure of her life. Her eyes met Jamie's.

Nothing is impossible, Daisy's voice sang inside her head.

Together on his computer, his shoulder nearly touching hers, they filled out the police report, and then she borrowed his phone and called her insurance company.

When she hung up, she was beaming. "They'll cover everything, even the costs involved in getting my passport replaced. They are being extraordinarily generous." She couldn't resist telling him how much they had offered her. "Shopping just became a lot more fun!"

But her confidence flagged a touch as their driver dropped them off on Fifth Avenue, arguably the most exclusive—and expensive—

shopping area in the world. As they joined the throngs of people enjoying the early-summer warmth and strolling the famous street, familiar names vied for her attention: Tiffany, Gucci, Versace, Hugo Boss, Luis Vuitton.

"Isn't there a Woolmart?" she asked Jamie, only partly kidding. She was getting a *Who do you think you are?* feeling. Glancing in the windows, she doubted, even with the insurance money, if she could afford a pair of socks on this block.

Jamie looked at her and smiled. "What do they sell? Wool?"

He was teasing her. It felt nice, but he wasn't getting the point.

"Look, I just need a few things, temporarily. This seems—"

"Fun?" he suggested.

Fun. A reminder of her goal for the day. A reminder of the new her. But new her or old her, she was going to have to be careful not to get carried away.

"There's nothing fun about bankruptcy," she said firmly. She stopped at the window of a jewelry store, and looked at the watches on display. She gasped. One of them was worth more than a hundred thousand dollars! And it looked quite a bit like the one on Jamie's wrist.

This suddenly didn't feel fun. Not at all. She felt so far out of her depth, she could soon drown.

As if sensing her sudden discomfort, Jamie swept his hand toward the rings that were displayed next to the watch.

"Which one do you like?"

They were obviously engagement rings, diamonds winking and blinking as the morning sun hit them. "That one," she said. It was as different as the sun was to the moon to the small promise ring Devon had once given her.

And perhaps, unfolding without her awareness, she had become as different from that long-ago girl as the choice of that ring would indicate. The thought was vaguely unsettling, but she shook it off and reminded herself of her goal to just let go, have some fun and relax a bit.

Jamie bent nearer to have a closer look. "You have good taste."

She looked at the discreet price tag displayed beside the box. "What kind of man would spend that on a ring?" she gasped, shocked.

"One who is very much in love?"

She slid him a look. Did he have a secret romantic side, then?

He took her elbow and steered her away from the jewelry store window and through the crowds.

"My sister recommended this place," he said and stopped at the black-painted door of a posh storefront. He opened the door, placed his hand on the small of her back and thrust her through it as if he sensed her desire to bolt.

Jessica stood there, letting her eyes adjust to the light. The space looked like a hybrid between a living room and a boutique. It looked expensive. It even *smelled* expensive.

And here came the saleslady who looked more like a wealthy heiress than a clerk. She was dressed in understated elegance, a single string of pearls at her neck, her makeup and hair and manicure absolutely perfect.

Jessica braced herself, ready to get kicked out. But then she could feel Jamie's presence behind her, and his hand resting on her shoulder, that solid warmth reminding her she was not only not alone, but also that she had a great guide for navigating his world.

"We're looking for Meredith," he told the woman.

"I'm Meredith."

"My sister, Sarah Stately, recommended you."

"I adore Sarah!"

"Don't we all?" he said dryly, "My friend here, Jessica Winton, is in New York for a few days and has had all her luggage stolen."

Meredith turned to her, and the genuine sympathy Jessica saw in her face belied whatever she had expected from the big-city shopping experience.

"You'll need absolutely everything." She couldn't hide her delight.

"Just for a few days," Jessica said quickly, resisting the temptation to go and start turning over price tags.

"I love your jacket. Clarion? The Canadian designer? You're Canadian, aren't you? I recognize the accent."

Jessica nodded. "The Clarion was a splurge," she said as a hint the jacket wasn't in her regular price range.

"Can I just say, that even though I love it, it seems, um, a bit mature. How old are you?"

"Twenty-six. I am here on business, so I need

items that are appropriate." She wanted to add, *and not too expensive,* but she'd wait until Jamie was out of hearing.

"Got it. You are safe with me." Meredith stood back, tapped a manicured finger against her lip. "You are going to be a dream to work with. Look at that figure."

Jamie seemed to take it as an instruction. He looked at her, she blushed. She looked at him, he blushed. That super suave man blushed! It was one of the most endearing things Jessica had ever seen.

He looked hastily to his expensive watch. "If an hour will work, I'll just duck out…"

Jessica felt oddly abandoned. Had she really thought he would stay? He was a busy man, and important. He wouldn't have time for something so frivolous as all this.

"You're not going anywhere," Meredith told him firmly. "We'll need your opinion if we want to get it just right."

Jessica shot Jamie a look. His mouth fell open, and then he slammed it shut. He ran a hand through the silver of his hair. Obviously, he was not used to being ordered about by a saleslady, no matter how high-end the shop.

But when he looked at Jessica, something shifted in his face. His colossal composure was rattled, but only briefly. He cocked his head at her, and then lifted a shoulder.

He was staying!

Jessica felt like a deer caught in headlights. When she had originally assumed he would stay, she hadn't considered modeling outfits for him. She supposed he would take out his phone and settle in one of those deep leather chairs at the front of the store.

It was a nightmare. Or a dream. She wasn't sure which.

Meredith showed her to the change rooms. Actually, more like a change *suite.* They entered a private enclave with a sitting area and a change room bigger than her bedroom in the tiny cottage she had in the yard behind her parents' house. It was certainly more well-appointed than her own lodgings, which suddenly seemed to lean more toward shabby than chic.

"In you go," Meredith said.

"But I haven't even looked at any clothes," Jessica protested.

"I'm going to choose things for you." She wagged a finger at her. "No dull colors. No safe but boring styles. No clothing that does not show off that super figure of yours!"

Jessica looked down at herself with a frown. Super figure? In Timber Falls they called it skinny. Still, it had made Jamie blush. She shot him a look. *Rescue me*, but apparently he was all done rescuing her for the time being. Because he wagged his eyebrows wickedly at her when Meredith mentioned her super figure, and then sank down in one of the chairs and pulled out his phone.

He could have had the decency to look a little uncomfortable—he was a man in a woman's clothing store, after all—but he looked terribly at home.

Jessica went in the change room and Meredith slipped in with her, closed the door and studied her. "Did you lose everything?"

"Everything. My luggage was stolen from me at the airport."

"So, you don't even have makeup?"

This said with a faint shudder, as if no makeup was a catastrophe beyond measure.

"No lingerie? Pajamas?

"Everything's gone."

"How many days do we need to get you sorted for?"

"Three," Jessica said, firmly. "If I can get my temporary passport, or travel documents, I'll be here for the three days I originally planned. But just in case it's a bit longer, I'll need things I can mix and match for slightly different looks."

"We'll get you fixed up. It may be a blessing in disguise. I'm going to send my assistant to get you some makeup. Your face is amazing. I can't wait to show you. It's going to be a makeover."

"Um, I'm not sure—"

"Your current bra, by the way, is a disaster," Meredith said.

"Pardon?"

"You'll see what I mean when I bring you a good one. Do you mind if I measure you?"

"Yes, I mind!" She crossed her arms defensively over her chest.

Meredith sighed. "All right, just give me a size then."

Jessica did. "And nothing fancy," she whispered, so that Jamie, sitting just outside the door, couldn't hear her. "I don't like underwires in my bra. And I don't like lace on my underwear, at all."

Meredith was looking mutinous.

"It's scratchy!"

Meredith left, and Jessica sank down on the Cleopatra-style pink tufted chaise longue. What had she just let herself in for? Another woman was choosing underwear for her. It was appalling. She should have protested more strenuously, instead of agreeing to be Meredith's hostage.

Shoot, she'd forgotten to mention that all important word. *Budget.* She looked at the ceiling. She'd worry about that later, when it came time to make final selections. She'd have to put her foot down then.

Jamie waited until Jessica had closed the change room door after Meredith left, then got up from his chair quietly and followed the sales associate out into the store.

"Can I get you to take the tags off things before you bring them in to her? I want her to get what she wants, and not be influenced by the price."

Jamie told himself that giving this instruction to the sales associate was why he had stayed. But it was a lie. There was something about being a witness to Jessica discovering some of the treasures of being in New York that he found himself unable to resist.

"At the end, if it could add up to her insurance settlement that would be great." He named the amount. "I'll look after the difference, if you can slip me a second bill."

What on earth was he doing?

"Love that!" Meredith said, grinning at him, a delighted coconspirator. She held up two dresses. "Which one do you think she would pick?"

One dress was a subtle gray pinstripe with straight lines and a longish skirt. The other was a sundress style with a full skirt. It was white with huge red poppies all over it.

"She'd go for the gray," he said. "Very businesslike."

"That's what I thought, too," Meredith said, and with a wide wink at him, hung the gray dress back up on the rack. "This other dress can be for business, too, with the right sweater and shoes. What do you think of this one?"

And so, somehow he ended up being on Jessica's personal shopping team. It was all fun and games until they came to the underwear section.

Meredith, unabashed, held up a pair of shapeless beige panties. "What do you think?"

He didn't want to be thinking about Jessica's panties, obviously!

"This is what she told me she wanted," Meredith said with barely concealed scorn.

Somehow, it made him feel oddly sad for Jessica that she didn't celebrate her femininity. On the other hand, if she did? Danger zone! He had to remove himself from this situation.

Meredith smiled at him, held up another pair.

He felt his mouth go dry. Thankfully, his phone pinged. He glanced at it. Not at all urgent. But he wagged the phone at Meredith, anyway. "I have to take this."

"Chicken," she mouthed at him, adding a generous supply of froth and film to the already gigantic pile over her arm. "Okay," she sang, "this will get us started."

You had to like a woman who loved her job.

"I haven't had a chance to tag these yet," Meredith said to Jessica as she went through the door of the change room. "I'm raiding our brand-new summer stock, just for you."

"But I need to know—"

The door closed on Jessica's protest, which Meredith must have managed to assuage, because Jessica emerged from the change room in the first outfit. It was the poppy-covered white sundress and she looked absolutely stunning.

If he was not mistaken, she had makeup on. It was subtle and yet the changes to her face were extraordinary. Her eyes looked huge, her cheekbones high and sculpted, her mouth a sultry pout of pure temptation. Her hair had been put up in casual knot, instead of clipped back, and tendrils were escaping and curling wildly around her face.

Despite the sophisticated woman-of-the-world look of the clothes, Jessica looked as shy as a young woman going on her first date.

Meredith had paired the dress with a short white cashmere sweater and white high heels, and the look was professional, yet hinted at a playful side at the same time.

"Give a twirl," Meredith ordered. "You have to see the movement in that skirt."

Jamie wasn't sure if he was ready for the movement in that skirt! Jessica hesitated.

"Pretend you are someone else," Meredith advised. "Elise Hollander on the red carpet."

Jessica hesitated, and then obviously made a decision to get in the spirit of things. She put a hand on her hip and cocked it. She twirled.

He expected she might be awkward, but nothing could have been further from the truth. She was as graceful as a ballerina, and her legs were toned, tanned and looked a mile long as the skirt swirled around them. He was pretty sure he caught a glimpse of a pair of panties that were about the furthest thing from boring beige that a man could imagine.

She finished her twirl, set her legs wide apart, put her hand back on her cocked hip and winked at him.

"Fun, flirty and youthful," Meredith declared approvingly. "Yes or no?"

Jessica held his gaze. He nodded his head, unable to speak.

Next she came out in a straight-lined plaid skirt, that should have looked librarian—or bookstore owner appropriate—paired with a pair of stilettos and a loose white blouse that was, by design, semitransparent. He could see a lacy outline beneath it. It was about the sexiest thing he had ever seen.

"These shoes…" she said hesitantly.

Shoes?

"Are perfect," he growled, without even looking at them.

Meredith was an absolute wizard at her job. The clothes she had chosen showed off Jessica's amazingly lithe but sexy figure. Jessica made the transformation from a small-town girl to a supermodel before his very eyes.

He loved seeing the change in her. It wasn't just the clothing, though obviously the cut of expensive clothes made a huge difference, and obviously Meredith had supplied a little something that had transformed Jessica's somewhat athletic figure into something far more beguiling.

With each outfit change, Jessica's confidence grew, her hips swinging, her eyes glowing with a soft luster as she began to unveil who she really was, certainly to him, but also to herself. By the time she tried on the last outfit, she was reveling in her femininity, enjoying the effect it was having on him.

He couldn't believe he was disappointed when Meredith opened the change room door, and announced, "Last one."

Jessica emerged in a dress that was light blue, a confection of gauze and spiderwebs. The dress clung in all the right places, and it made her seem mysterious and alluring.

"I certainly don't need the cocktail dress. I don't even know why I tried it on."

But the expression on her face belied the words she had just spoken. She *loved* that dress.

"You're in New York City!" Meredith said. "Surely you're going to go out for a gorgeous dinner at Le Bernardin and take in a Broadway show."

Jessica cast him an uncertain look. "I don't think there's anything like that on the agenda, is there?"

Jamie could hear the wistfulness in her tone, and just like that, Le Bernardin and a Broadway show was on the agenda. He was being bewitched!

He had to stop it, though. He'd turn her over to an assistant for the rest of the day. Get his head on straight—and the boundaries back in place—before he took her out for dinner and a show.

Jessica cast a glance at herself in the bank of mirrors. "It's going to be impossible to decide what to take. Not this, obviously."

"That one, especially. You should take it all," he said.

"I couldn't possibly. You think this one? Really?"

"Absolutely that one," he said.

"I guess find me the price on this one," Jessica said. "And the white-and-red sundress. I'll figure out from there if I can afford anything else."

"Let me figure out what it would cost if you took it all," Meredith said smoothly, "and if you can't handle it, we'll start editing."

"But—"

Meredith swept up all the clothes and left them.

"I feel like Cinderella," Jessica said, sinking into the chair beside him. The dress hitched up on a slender leg. He tried not to look. Failing in that, he tried not to be obvious about looking.

"But it's just about midnight. The glass slipper falls off, and I see what it all costs. I probably can't even afford one thing from here."

He looked at his watch so she wouldn't see the pleasure in his eyes that he was going to play a part in her fairy tale.

Not the prince part, of course. Though something about seeing her in all those clothes could tempt any man to play that role, even one as cynical about fairy tales as him.

Meredith came back. She held out a piece of paper to Jessica.

Jessica took it, looked at it, and blinked. "Oh,"

she said. "It's so much less than I expected. Still, I don't need two skirts. So, I should probably take out the pencil-line one and keep the navy pants."

Meredith snatched the paper back from her. "I forgot to add Sarah's preferred customer discount."

Jessica took back the paper with the adjusted price. Her mouth fell open with shocked surprise.

"All right," she cried, beaming, "I'll take it all!"

As Meredith handled the transaction—giving the one bill to Jessica and putting the real amount on Jamie's credit card, Jamie realized this was probably the most duplicitous thing he had ever done. But Jessica was absolutely radiant.

"I'll pay you back, of course. The insurance representative said I'll have some money by this afternoon."

How could something feel both so very wrong and so very right at the same time?

When they left the store, Jessica was wearing the brand-new sundress. Jamie couldn't help but notice that, in a city where no one paid any attention to anyone else, Jessica was receiving subtle—and deeply appreciative glances—from the men of New York.

A man on a construction site whistled at her. Jamie threw him a warning glance, and then noticed Jessica was blushing as though she had been propositioned.

How could he turn her over to an assistant when it was so complicated? Jessica now *looked* like a sophisticated woman of the world. But she was the furthest thing from that. He couldn't just cast her out on her own. A still small voice, somewhere in the region of his heart, whispered to him, *Admit it, pal, you don't want to.*

CHAPTER SIX

WALKING DOWN FIFTH AVENUE, with Jamie beside her, his arms laden with the parcels he had refused to let her carry, Jessica felt amazing. Like a sleeping princess who had been brought to life.

Not with a kiss, of course, though the thought made her take a quick look at the sensuous turn of his mouth and realize that kissing Jamie Gilbert-Cooper was not as impossible as it had seemed just this morning. Their worlds were intersecting.

The funny thing about the impromptu makeover, her astonishing new look and awesome new wardrobe was that she hadn't felt out of her element.

As Meredith had expertly applied that makeup—making Jessica's eyes look huge and dark, her cheekbones look amazing, her mouth look sensuous and faintly sultry—Jessica had not felt like Cinderella, dressing up as someone she was not. She had felt more like duckling to swan.

With each stroke of Meredith's hand on the makeup brush, and with each outfit she had tried on, something about herself, that had always been there, was being revealed. When she had stood before Jamie in that final outfit, the cocktail dress, Jessica had felt as though she had become who she really was.

At that time she hadn't known what that dress was worth—still didn't know the prices of individual items for that matter—but the look on his face had made her decide it was worth its weight in gold.

"So," Jamie suggested, as they exited Hennessey's, "let's go look after things at the Canadian Consulate office, and then I'll surprise you for lunch."

Jessica was not really sure if it was Jamie's presence, or her own growing confidence, but things went far better than she had anticipated. Though they could not replace her passport immediately, they would treat her case as urgent, and contact her through Jamie as soon as they had temporary documents available so she could travel.

Unfortunately, until they had completely verified her identity, they could not give a photo ID.

Which meant she still could not get a hotel. It meant she would be staying with Jamie one more night, at least. She was appalled at how thrilled she was by that!

After that, the rest of the day was a whirl of delight: the Russian Tea Room for champagne high tea, a stroll through Central Park, where they paused and watched little boys—and one little girl—race remote control boats on the reservoir. The little girl kept ramming the boats around her, and then giggling fiendishly.

"Was that you as a little girl?" Jamie asked.

"No, I'm afraid I've always been the good girl." Then she realized how it sounded and she blushed.

He took in her blush, and the smallest smile, just a touch wicked, crossed his features, as if he were having wayward thoughts about rectifying that.

It occurred to her she would let him!

"What were you like as a little boy?" she said, to ease some of the sudden tense awareness of each other that tinged the warm summer air around them.

"Pick one," he said, nodding toward the boys.

She studied them for a moment, and then pointed to a solemn-looking boy who appeared to be dismantling his boat to diagnose a problem. Jamie laughed. He was one of those men who threw back his head to laugh. A light came on in his face, making him—impossibly—even more attractive. His laughter was so deep and rich and genuine, that Jessica noticed it brought smiles to the faces of those passing by, New Yorkers generally famous for being oblivious to one another.

"Maybe more like that one," he said, pointing to a lad whose hair was going every which way, and who had his pants rolled up and was in the water up to his ankles. "If he catches a frog, tomorrow it's going in the desk of the girl he secretly loves."

The thought of Jamie secretly loving someone sent tingles up and down her spine. "You don't seem like that at all," she said hastily, not sure if she was talking about the little boy, or the ability to secretly love someone. She remembered when they had looked at that expensive ring together she had wondered if he had a secret romantic side. It was dangerous—and thrilling—to be thinking of him in such a personal way.

"Like most boys, I've outgrown my desire to put frogs in girl's drawers."

The way he said *drawers* made her think of her sexy new underwear, and from the wicked look on his face, that was exactly what he intended. Jessica was fairly certain that the only part of that equation he had lost interest in was the frog part.

"My mother claims every gray hair on her head was caused by my *shenanigans*—her word not mine—between the ages of two and eighteen."

"Ha! I think gray hair may be hereditary in your family." He rewarded her with a smile, but then she remembered what he had told her last night. "The shenanigans stopped at eighteen because of the death of your father, didn't they?"

He hesitated, and looked off into the distance. "I was suddenly the man of the family. It was a role nothing in my life, to that point, had prepared me for."

Unlike her, shrinking away from life when Devon had died, she had a feeling he had handled it differently.

"You rose to it, didn't you?" she asked softly.

She laid her fingertips on his forearm, where his shirt was rolled up. She thought he might pull away, but he didn't. If anything, the touch connected them at a deeper level.

"I think I pretty much sucked at it," he said, some emotion in the sudden hoarseness of his voice.

"I don't believe that," she said firmly.

He looked at her, deeply, as if there was something in those simple words he wanted to hang on to. "It was just a tough time. Along with the shock of sudden loss—he had a heart attack—I was suddenly plunged into the world of adult responsibility. He left some insurance and savings, but for a while I wondered if I could find a way for my mom to have a home again and let my sister go to college as she had always dreamed."

"You did find a way?"

"I did," he said.

"You don't sound as proud of yourself as you should."

He lifted a shoulder. "I managed the *things* that they needed. But I couldn't take the pain away."

"You're very hard on yourself," she said softly.

"I had a sense of failing them almost every day."

She could tell a man like him would not like anything he perceived as failure. She knew it was probably uncharacteristic for him to reveal something like this of himself, and she could feel his trust in her trickle warmly down her spine.

"I think you held yourself to an impossible standard."

"Do you, now?" he asked softly.

She nodded, and he seemed to take that in, before he shrugged it off, as if it was absolution he felt he was undeserving of.

"If you ask my sister, it soured me."

"You don't seem sour!" She finally, reluctantly, took her hand away from his arm.

He smiled at her. "Thanks. Sarah thinks everyone should be happily married and producing children, like her, otherwise it is not a life well lived. She says all that shouldering the family responsibility so young killed that for me."

"And did it?" Jessica whispered.

"Oh, yeah. She has gone as far as to call me hedonistic."

"That seems mean. After all you've done for her."

"We like to tease each other. I call her DD for Domestic Diva."

Jessica liked these little glimpses into who Jamie was. She liked it that he and his sister teased each other. Still, she felt a need to defend him. "Anyway, you are not! Hedonistic."

"Yes, ma'am, I am. Self-centered and selfish. I work hard. I play harder. I'm allergic to domestic activities and responsibilities, hence the reason no turkey has ever filled my oven."

Despite the lightness of Jamie's tone, it was a warning to her, that was clear. He had already told her he saw her as a picket fence kind of girl, and he was letting her know he did not fit that kind of dream.

He was painting a picture of himself as the quintessential playboy.

And yet, looking at him, his shirt open at the throat, his sleeves rolled up, the sun on his silver hair and the exquisite lines of his face, she didn't feel he had shown her one sign that he was selfish or self-centered. Still, she was aware a girl could change her dreams to fit his.

A girl could loosen her hold on the concept of *forever* and be willing to just take whatever he offered. It might actually be fun to not be the good girl, for once. She was in New York. She was a long way from home. Who would ever know if she had a little fling with a sexy man? She experienced a shiver of pure *wanting* when she thought of Jamie in those terms, when she thought of his lips claiming hers, his hands...

Stop it! She ordered herself.

Given their circumstances—his potential to be her boss, her forced stay in his quarters—she was entertaining very perilous thoughts, indeed.

When they turned away from the young boaters to walk again, she went over on her ankle ever so slightly because of the unfamiliar shoes. Despite the fact she knew she was flirting in general and flirting with danger in particular, when he reached out to steady her, she did not return his steadying arm to him when she should have.

No, she looped her arm though his—felt the surge of delight at being linked to him—as they moved along the pathway toward his building.

"I hope you don't mind," she said. "I'm not used to the shoes. I'm going to skin my nose if I don't have you to lean on."

He looked down at her for a long moment. He looked as if he wanted to warn her not to play with fire. Instead, he took a deep breath. "We wouldn't want you to skin a cute little nose like that," he said.

Cute. He thought she was cute. Or that her

nose was. Cute was a long way from pretty. Or gorgeous. Or beautiful.

And yet she liked it very much that he thought her nose was cute.

And then he started humming, *lean on me*, and Jessica was glad she had silenced her good girl because she was not sure she had ever experienced a more perfect moment than that one, walking through Central Park on a sun-drenched day, in her new dress, with a gorgeous man on her arm.

One perfect moment was determined to follow another. She wore her new cocktail dress for the most exquisite dinner she had ever had. Whether it was the food, or Jamie's company she wasn't sure. He was so at ease in every situation, radiating confidence and good humor. Maybe his sister was right about him! He certainly seemed practiced at entertaining the opposite sex. Conversation with him seemed so easy. They talked about everything: books, recent movies, music they liked, travels they had experienced. Her travels were limited—only Copenhagen—but Jamie had been many places, both professionally and personally.

His anecdotes revealed him as a man with a rich sense of humor and a great verve for life.

He had gotten tickets to *The Phantom of the Opera*, which he told her was the longest running show in Broadway history. She was thrilled. But somehow, just as thrilling as going in to the show was standing in line with him at the Majestic Theatre, and seeing the admiring gazes he garnered. Jessica realized she was very much enjoying being mistaken for a couple.

She was also enjoying the sheer variety of the crowd. There was everything here from elderly couples to families, and even a school group.

"The variety of what people are wearing is amazing," she whispered to Jamie. It was true, there was everything from men in tropical print Hawaiian shirts and shorts, to women in evening gowns.

"The really dressed up ones are tourists," he whispered back.

"Am I overdressed?" she asked, feeling a bit of the magic slip away. "I haven't had on anything this fancy since my prom."

He cast an appreciative look over her, long enough and male enough that she felt herself starting to blush.

"You," he said, softly, "are perfect. Ravishing."

Just like that, the magic was back. Jamie Gilbert-Cooper thought she was ravishing!

When she shivered from the gruesome makeup on the phantom, Jamie assumed she was cold, and she found his suit jacket settling around her shoulders. It felt so nice that she did not correct him.

Jessica was not sure what she had been expecting from the show, but it was incredibly sensuous in places, and terrifying in others. When the chandelier "fell" into the audience she shrieked very unbecomingly. Jamie's hand found hers and then he lifted her hand to his lips and kissed her wrist.

Jessica was pretty sure her heart stop beating. She turned and looked at him, and very deliberately, he lifted her wrist to his lips again and kissed it.

It was not, to be sure, a wildly passionate kiss. It was more a reassurance: See? Nothing to be afraid of. I'm right here beside you.

And nothing felt frightening after that except maybe the wild beating of a heart going down a pathway it had never been down before.

* * *

Jessica Winton was not his type, Jamie told himself, for the umpteenth time. She was a small-town girl in a big-city world. Even dressed up in *that* dress, even with her makeup applied expertly, even with her hair piled on top of her head in a sophisticated bun, there was a quality about her that was wholesome. It was not exactly naive, and yet it was not worldly either.

Whatever that quality was it had coaxed him to tell her about the death of his father, and to confide in her the effect that event had had on him and the course his life had taken.

He wasn't accustomed to sharing confidences, so he told himself he'd intended it as a kind of warning to her, probably because he could feel the attraction lighting up between them.

I am not the settling down kind of guy.

And yet, no matter what reason he had confided in her, after he had felt oddly lighter, as if he had been carrying a burden he didn't even know he carried. The way she had looked at him, the way her hand had rested so lightly on his arm, had made him feel as if the power of the sun had intensified.

Now, it felt as if he was seeing his world

through her eyes, and it was hard not to find her delight in things that he took for granted contagious.

When she screamed when the chandelier fell, it was the most natural thing in the world to take her hand in his.

But what made him lift it to his lips and kiss the inside of her wrist? He told himself it was not a romantic gesture, but a chivalrous one.

I'm here. Don't be afraid.

And yet, when she went still beside him, when he turned to acknowledge the wideness of her eyes with a steady look, he was not so sure that anything had ever felt quite so good as being there for her.

So, he kissed the underside of her wrist again, before tucking her hand into his side. He resisted the temptation to stroke the inside of her palm with his thumb, because that would take things to a whole different level that would give an entirely different message than *I'm here for you, your protector in the big city.*

Still, with her hand in his, it felt like a good thing he had seen *Phantom* before, because he was so conscious of her beside him, that not a single thing that unfolded onstage pierced that awareness.

He knew the impossibility of flagging a cab after a show had just gotten out, so he had arranged for a driver to be waiting for them.

He should have thought of this when he was laying tender kisses on the inside of her wrist: she was coming home with him.

She looked adorable snuggled under his jacket in the back seat. He moved as far away from her as the car seat would allow. He could see kissing her wrist in the darkness of the theater, suddenly and with excruciating clarity for what it had been: *temporary insanity.*

"Would you like a drink?" he asked her.

Now what part of that would move them back toward sanity?

"I'd usually say no," she said, "but how often am I going to be able to sit in a limo on Broadway in New York City having a drink?"

"What would you like?"

When she hesitated, he could tell she rarely drank. She didn't even know what to ask for. She must have realized what her hesitation was telling him, because she said, breezily, "Whatever I had yesterday is fine."

Just yesterday? She had only been part of his life since yesterday? How was that possible when everything seemed so changed?

He poured her a little sip of cognac, and poured himself a more bracing one. Why was he acting like a man under threat?

Thankfully, they made the trip from Broadway to his apartment in about twelve minutes.

He brooded all the way back to his place. He'd let his guard down. He'd wanted to be a good host, and try to erase her awful first impression of New York. He'd felt, quite naturally, protective of her. But he had crossed boundaries.

He'd gone shopping with her. That was an activity reserved for people in committed relationships, now that he thought about it. Why hadn't he thought about that sooner?

He'd taken her for lunch and supper. He'd strolled through Central Park with her. He'd taken her to *The Phantom of the Opera*.

No wonder she was looking at him with *that* terrifying expression on her face.

He'd been treating this whole day as if it was some kind of date. She was in a vulnerable position. He might end up being her boss.

He contemplated that.

Her boss.

One day with her had him feeling as if his whole reality was shifting. What if she decided to take this job? His life would be brushing up against hers, day in and day out...

"I think the car has stopped," she told him. Her voice was husky. Her eyes were half-lidded.

He scrambled out of the car, and managed, just barely, not to bolt up to the safety of his apartment, leaving her to find her own way.

Running away was not an option.

For Pete's sake, he lectured himself, he had dated some of the most desirable women on the planet. This little lady from Lumber—no, Timber—Falls was not a threat to him. He held out his hand to her to help her out of the car.

The dress slid up, revealing a mouthwatering glimpse of legs that went on forever. He let go of her hand as soon as he had extracted her from the car. He stood as far away from her on the elevator as he could. When the door opened he managed, just barely, to let her out before him. And then he got out, and went by her, making a beeline for the sanctuary of his bedroom.

"Jamie?"

He turned and looked at her.

Her makeup was a little smudged. Her hair was falling out of the twist it had been in. While he watched, she shrugged out of his jacket, revealing herself to him: the long legs, the bodice that clung like mist, the gentle curve of her shoulders.

His mouth felt dry.

"You'll be wanting this," she said.

He stared at her. Her voice had that same husky note to it that he had noticed in the car.

Note to self, he told himself, *do not give Jessica Winton cognac ever again.*

If he told her to just put the jacket down, she was going to *know* she was having an effect on him.

It seemed imperative that she not know that, that he maintain the balance of power.

He sauntered back to her, held out his hand for the jacket.

She placed it in his hand, and then moved in close to him.

"I can't thank you enough for today," she said. "It is the closest I've ever come to having a perfect day."

He reflected on that. They hadn't done anything very spectacular. He, on the other hand, had done spectacular things. He had experienced days that could be called perfect; skiing in St. Moritz, snorkeling off the Kona Coast, trekking in South America. He had been to the final game of the World Series, not once, but twice, and been on a photo safari in Mozambique.

And yet, looking at Jessica, it suddenly seemed as if she was correct. Everything else in his history paled in comparison to today.

She moved toward him. Her intent was obvious. She was going to kiss him. He presumed on the cheek, one of those nice *thank you* busses that his mother gave him after they had experienced a lovely outing.

He wasn't quite sure what changed: the position of his cheek or her intent.

Because the sweetness of Jessica Winton's lips missed his cheek entirely. And connected with his mouth.

For the first fragment of the first second, he might have had the power to move.

But then he was lost.

Her mouth was as sweet as a strawberry that had ripened under the sun. Her kiss transported him to the mountains from where she came. She had a taste to her, what he imagined the fine spray of water cascading over a rock would taste like.

He had deluded himself that he had some knowledge of what a perfect moment was.

Because it was not until the softness of her lips sought his that Jamie knew, fully, completely, unequivocally, exactly what perfect was.

He was in the thrall of something now. For a man who had always prided himself on self-control, he would chide himself—later—for how quickly his had dissolved.

Because suddenly it was just him and her.

The whole world was only him and only her.

There was no tony address in Central Park South telling him he'd arrived, there was no thrum of the city outside his window, there was no great job, holidays to plan for, new and heady successes to achieve.

It felt as if he had lived all of that for this single arrival.

Her.

Jessica's mouth opened against his, soft, moist, beckoning him yet deeper into the enchantment that was her.

Far in the back of his brain, some rational part,

called to him. Wrong time. Wrong place. Wrong woman.

Wrong. Wrong. Wrong.

But the primal part of his brain was having none of it, crying, just as loudly.

Right. Right. Right.

He lifted his hands to the sides of her face, bracketed it, looked into her wide eyes for permission, which he found. He dropped his mouth over hers, explored the willing, beguiling sweetness with increasing urgency.

He let his hands move, he let them tangle in the silk of her hair, and he pulled her more closely to him.

It was her whimper of pure pleasure, discovery, someone who had never quite experienced this depth of passion before, that brought Jamie harshly to his senses. When she had told him about her fiancé, for one crazy moment in time he had *wanted* this. He had wanted to be the one to awaken this in her. That was why he hadn't backed away from her invitation when he should have.

It was greedy and selfish and unconscionable. He had known this woman just a little over twenty-four hours. Of course sometimes, in his world, things progressed quickly.

But not in hers.

He yanked back from her and stepped away, watching her, utterly appalled with himself. She was not a woman from his world. She was not anything like any woman he had ever taken out before.

As he watched, he could see her breath was rising, moving too quickly in and out. Her eyes were wide. Her lips looked thoroughly kissed.

Both her eyes and those altogether too tempting lips begged for more.

"I'm sorry," he managed to choke out.

"Sorry?" she whispered, as though he had insulted her.

"Yes, sorry," he reiterated firmly. "I can't imagine what I was thinking. That was completely inappropriate."

She nodded, once, biting the lushness of that lower lip.

He was pretty sure, watching her work that lip, that his strength had never been tested quite like this before.

"Good night," he said, his voice a rasp of pure need. He turned away from her before he broke and ran back to her, swept her up in his arms, finished what he had so foolishly started.

He managed to get in his bedroom and close the door. He leaned against it and shut his eyes.

But it didn't matter that his eyes were shut. All he could see was her lips.

CHAPTER SEVEN

JESSICA FOUND HER way to her room in a daze. She realized she was humming "The Point of No Return" from the musical. But when she lay down in her bed, Daisy's song replaced it inside her head. "Nothing is Impossible."

She realized, mutinously, she did not care if Jamie thought that kiss was inappropriate. For her, it had been the perfect ending to an absolutely perfect day. She hoped she would dream of his lips on hers, and she did wake in the morning with a lovely sense of bliss.

She chose her outfit carefully from her purchases from Hennessey's. Today would be all business and she dressed for that in the pencil line skirt, the white blouse, the flat shoes. But at the last moment, she undid a button one daring level lower than she normally would have, and she left her hair loose.

Jamie was up, the breakfast selection already put out on the island. He took in her loose hair and the button position on her blouse and his eyes darkened. Then he looked at her lips—lightly outlined with gloss, as Meredith had showed her—and his gaze lingered for a full two seconds before he looked at his phone.

"Big day today," he said, apparently studying their agenda.

Jessica realized Jamie was as awkward with her as if something quite a bit more substantial than a kiss had occurred between them. She probably should have felt some shame—after all, she had instigated that "inappropriate" kiss with a man who could be her boss—but she felt no remorse at all.

In fact, she was a bit delighted that she, an unsophisticated woman from a small town, had managed to rattle the super suave Jamie Gilbert-Cooper. She made a point of "accidentally" touching his hand as she reached for a bagel. He yanked his own away as if he had been burned.

Before they were done eating breakfast, a courier arrived, with funds for her from the insurance company, and a temporary replacement for her credit card.

Her whole world felt rosy!

She tried to repay him, on the spot, for the

shopping trip, but he told her to hang on to her cash, in case she saw something else she wanted, and to send him an e-transfer when she got home.

They took the car to his office, which was in the Financial District, and he pointed out the sights to her, his tone conversational, but in a deliberately tour guide kind of way. They whisked by the statues of the *Charging Bull* on Wall Street, and the *Fearless Girl*. He pointed out the 9/11 Memorial Plaza, and Museum, and Saint Paul's Chapel.

And then they were at his office. From the moment she entered the doors, she realized this sumptuous space, with its incredible view toward the Empire State Building could be her office one day, too.

The day went by in a whirl. It was as unlike yesterday as a day could be. Jamie introduced her to his business world, and to what her future job might entail. It was unbelievably exciting: bringing her skill set with her bookstore to a wider application, which would include liaising with publishers and bookstores, and with bookstores and authors. It would include setting up events and seminars to help independent bookstore owners to achieve the same results she had.

She and Jamie had lunch with a publisher and an author. At first, she thought she would feel awkwardly out of her depth, but as soon as the talk turned to books and bookstores she was right at home. She had a growing sense, not just of being able to hold her own in this environment, but of being so at home with it. After lunch, they visited two bookstores who were current clients of JHA, and despite being in the middle of New York City, Jessica was, again, right at home.

This was her forte: bringing vibrancy and a sense of life and verve to a bookstore. She and the owners clicked immediately over their shared love of books, and the feeling that a bookstore should really be at the heart of any community.

She was aware, as the day went on, that the awkwardness that kiss had caused between her and Jamie dissipated somewhat. She was quite pleased to see a growing respect for her in his eyes.

But why was he surprised? Why had I been asked to consider the job if they didn't already know what my skill level was?

She brushed the question aside when Jamie

handed her his phone. "Canadian Consulate," he told her.

She took it and learned she would be issued temporary travel documents early tomorrow afternoon. It meant she could catch her return flight as scheduled tomorrow evening.

Why did she feel almost disappointed? She realized she felt as though she had just begun to explore this world, and that she didn't just want more, she felt as if she couldn't get enough.

It felt as if it was ending before it had really begun.

This could be my life, she thought.

"I'll be going home on schedule," she told him, keeping her tone deliberately neutral, as she handed him back his phone.

Something flashed across his handsome features that could have been regret. Or maybe it was relief.

"Is there anything you wanted to see before you go?"

"I have to see the New York Public Library," she told him, "nerd that I am."

He looked at her solemnly. "I don't think you're a nerd, at all." His eyes rested on her lips for a moment. "I have some things I have to do this afternoon. So, why don't I put the driver at your disposal, and you can take in whatever sights you want? I'll meet you back at the apartment and we'll figure out something truly spectacular for dinner for your last night here."

It was when she went out to the car that she realized, instead of reveling in the awkwardness she had made Jamie feel by kissing him, she should be thinking of a way to thank him for all he had done.

He had not just come to her rescue, he had completely turned a horrible situation around. When she thought back on this time in New York, the theft of her luggage would be just a hilarious footnote to what had been a wonderful time.

And maybe it was because the choice she had to make—about whether to accept the position or not—suddenly felt so overwhelming that she realized exactly how she could thank Jamie and get her own feet back on the ground at the same time.

She could give him, the man who had everything, the one thing he didn't have.

A sense of what a home could feel like. She

had money, she had a credit card and she knew exactly how she wanted to spend some of it.

Instead of asking the driver to take her to the New York Public Library, she asked, "Where do you buy food here? If you want to cook?"

An hour later she arrived back at Jamie's apartment with everything she needed to make the best home-cooked meal ever.

She had a moment's doubt, then. She suddenly felt foolish. Why would she think anything she could offer him could compete with the culinary delights that were just outside his door?

Well, unless she was planning on trying to put a prime rib roast down the in-sink garbage disposal, she was committed.

Jamie stepped off the elevator into his apartment and stopped short. Jessica was behind the island, tongue caught between her teeth, peeling potatoes. He was fairly certain a potato had never been peeled in this space before.

He sniffed the air. It smelled heavenly. Like roasting meat and pies. It smelled like coming home.

She glanced up at him and smiled tentatively. She had a bib apron that said *Life is Short, Lick the Spoon* on over that super sexy outfit she had worn today. How was it possible she looked even sexier?

"What are you doing?" he asked her, and heard the caution in his voice. "I thought you were going to the library."

"I decided that could wait. I wanted to thank you for all you've done for me. I tried to figure out what to give the man who had everything, and a home-cooked meal topped the list."

He contemplated that. She had given up one of the things she wanted to do most to give something to him.

He was unbelievably touched by that. Besides, what man wouldn't want to come home to something like this?

"I actually got to use the double ovens," she said, nodding at the pies cooling at her elbow. All of New York outside his door, and she was thrilled that she had used a double oven?

As Jamie looked at Jessica, he was aware of feeling a strange longing, a longing for the life he had not chosen. How easy it suddenly was to picture children tumbling across the room toward him, happy to see him, crying *Daddy.*

The vision was as shocking—and compelling—as imagining her in a field of lavender. What was it about this woman that so bewitched him? That made secrets he had kept, even from himself, thrust their way up to the surface?

Claim you have a meeting you forgot and get out of here, he ordered himself.

Instead, Jamie found himself drawn into the warmth she had created in his space. As he drew closer to her, he was acutely aware that the life he had chosen suddenly seemed empty—filled with things and lacking soul—and it made him feel alone in a way he had not felt before.

"What can I help with?" he asked gruffly, coming around to her side of the kitchen island, not wanting to reveal to her the full extent of the feelings clawing up through him.

"I've got an extra potato peeler."

How could that invitation possibly sound sexy? And dangerous? When he took off his suit jacket and joined her at the sink, he knew why it was both sexy and dangerous.

"Here," she said, "let's get an apron on you. It will protect your clothes."

"I don't have an apron," he protested, but she took a folded piece of cloth off the counter and shook it out.

"You do now."

What was this *let's* put the apron on? He had been dressing himself since he was two. Plus, she had obviously *planned* to get him involved, even knowing full well what had happened between them last night. But, no doubt on purpose, she had wisely chosen a very wholesome activity.

He should have backed away, but instead he ducked his head so that she could put the loop of the apron over it. She was so close. It reminded him of that kiss last night. It would be so easy to…

He steeled himself against unwholesome thoughts. They had no place in this most wholesome of activities.

He tilted his head down and read, upside down, the phrase on his apron. It said *I'm cute AND I can cook.*

"I think I got your apron," Jamie said. "This is a lie."

"Only half of it," she told him with a sassy grin.

Was she flirting with him? He frowned at her. Hadn't she got the memo? Flirting had no part in a wholesome activity!

Jessica went behind him and tied the apron securely. The apron snugging up against his waist and her hands at his back increased both the sense that there was potential here for unwholesomeness and the sense he had entered a scene of domestic bliss. She handed him a potato peeler.

"Your weapon," she told him.

He looked at her lips, her weapon. He turned quickly away from her, grabbed a large potato and focused furiously on removing the skin from it.

They were shoulder to shoulder. Her scent was blending with the smell of a roast cooking and pies cooling. Her hair was shiny and begged his fingers to tangle in it like they had last night. Who could have imagined peeling potatoes could be so much fun and such an exercise in discipline?

An hour later, they sat down at his dining room table to eat. The roast was overcooked and the potatoes were lumpy because she had not considered the possibility he would neither have milk to mash them, nor an implement created specifically for that purpose. The gravy had not thickened properly and the apple pie was sour enough to make him pucker.

"Well, that was a disaster," she said, sadly.

"Really?" he said. "I think it's easily one of the most exquisite meals I've ever eaten. With the best company."

"That's a lie," she said.

"Only half of it."

And there was the laughter, again, springing up so easily between them.

"So, it's your last night in New York. Is there anything I can do to make it special? To thank you for this?" He gestured at the table, littered with the remains of dinner.

Her eyes found his lips, and skittered away.

"No, no," she said hastily, "you don't have to thank me for this, this was to thank you. Oh, geez, I sound like those chipmunks who are always trying to outdo each other in politeness. *After you. No, after you, I insist.*"

He laughed at her great impression. "And then they end up fighting!" he reminded her.

And then they were both laughing at the absurdity of it.

"Come on," he coaxed her, "what's on your New York wish list?"

"Oh, no, I—"

"It's an order."

"Now you sound like Beast."

He cocked his head at her.

"As in *Beauty and the Beast*?"

"I'm not familiar with it."

"You are so! Belle is the town bookworm."

"Like you?"

She blushed. A man could live to make her blush. He made her tell him the whole story, pretending it was all new to him.

"I can't believe you've never seen that movie," she said when she had finished.

He laughed and sang, "'No one's as slick as Gaston, no one's as quick as Gaston—'"

She scowled at him. "Why did you let me go on and on about it?"

"You were so earnest. My sister made me watch that with her, over and over again, when she got chicken pox, not long after my dad died."

Jessica looked at him, and the loveliest smile tilted her lips. A man could live to make her smile. "And you think you failed in some way?" she asked softly.

And a man could live for that, too. For a sense of his flaws being filtered through a gentler, more forgiving light than the one he held on himself.

"Pick something," he insisted, now more determined than ever to give her some precious memory to take home with her, since, of course, he had no intention of giving in to the desire to do everything he did for her—for her blush, for her smile, for that light that came on in her eyes that made him feel ten feet tall and bulletproof.

She hesitated. "You'll think it's corny."

"Cornier than my apron?"

"Maybe."

"Try me."

"I wanted to go on the horse-drawn carriage through the park."

"You know, I've lived here all my life, and I've never done that."

"I told you, corny."

"I think it's about time I did," he told her softly. If his sister could see him pulling out his phone to check availability for the carriage ride tonight, she would no doubt repeat what she had said to him when he had texted her that first night that Jessica had arrived.

Who are you and what have you done with my brother?

He shushed that voice and pushed a single button to book the carriage ride. An hour later,

Jamie watched, amused, as Jessica introduced herself to the horse. She blew into his nose, and despite her beautiful clothes, she didn't even step back when he blew back on her. In fact, she threw back her head and laughed.

Jamie thought a world without her laughter to look forward to was going to feel empty in a way he had not realized the world could be empty just forty-eight hours ago.

"She knows horses," the carriage driver said approvingly.

"Do you?" Jamie asked Jessica.

"Oh, sure. Timber Falls is rural. I always had a pony when I was growing up. Horse-crazy teenager, all that stuff."

A reminder, as she settled in beside him, of what she was. *Wholesome.* Ponies and pies. Not the kind of woman a guy like him should tangle with any further than he already had. But what was he going to do? Jump off the carriage and tell her to have a good time, he had just thought of something he needed to do?

Surrender, he told himself.

This was about her. Not about him. She was here only a short time more. And then what?

Was she leaving forever? Or was she coming

back? Would she be working with him, day in and day out?

He took his place beside her in the carriage. He tried to keep some distance between them, but she shivered, and tonight he didn't have a jacket to put over her shoulders.

He surrendered yet again. He moved closer to her, throwing what he hoped was a companionable arm over her slim shoulders.

"What are your thoughts about the job?" he asked. It was a desperate and pathetically late effort to keep all of this in some way businesslike. That already seemed hopeless. But he had to try.

Jessica felt like Cinderella, with Jamie's arm around her shoulders, the steady clip-clop of the horse's hooves, dusk falling over Central Park. She felt as exquisitely alive as she had ever felt, as if the night air was creating tiny explosions of sensation against her skin.

She wished Jamie wouldn't have mentioned the job!

"I don't know yet," she said. "There's a lot to think about. It's not just my own business, though of course that is part of it. Who would look after it? And a big part of it is my mom and dad. They aren't old—both in their late fifties—and they're in good health and active, but they rely on me quite a bit."

"In what way?"

"Technology baffles them. I think I get a call or a visit once a day at the store with questions about their television, or their phones. Don't even get me going on their recent purchase of matching tablets!"

He laughed.

"My mom has taken to social media, though," she said ruefully.

Even as she said it, she realized these sounded like weak reasons to put a life on hold.

"I think they would want you to do what is best for you," he said.

"You're right, of course. If you met them, you would see that instantly."

Jamie Gilbert-Cooper meeting her parents? She couldn't imagine what circumstances that would cause these two very different worlds to collide.

A wedding, something sighed within her. She instantly banished the thought as both embarrassing and ridiculous. Despite feeling she *knew* Jamie, the truth was she did not. This sense of intimacy was because he had rescued her. He had invited her into his life. He had treated her like a princess. Conversation flowed easily between them. They laughed together. There was definitely chemistry!

All that was not a reason to start humming *someday my prince will come*, even if she was riding in a horse-drawn carriage!

It probably was showing her that Aubrey and Daisy were absolutely right: Jessica had made her world too small. Her reaction to this close proximity to such a confident, charming, gorgeous man was a result of not having nearly enough encounters with men of any sort.

Not since Devon had died. Not since the fiasco with Ralph in Copenhagen. Ralph should really serve as her lesson: her romantic notions could get her in trouble.

Though, a voice insisted on pointing out, Jamie was the opposite of Ralph. Her illusions about Ralph had collapsed as they had spent more time together. The more time she spent with Jamie, the more enamored she felt!

"You must be leaning one way or the other, though," he said. "The clients you met today loved you."

"Did they?"

"Unequivocally."

She wanted someone else to love her unequivo-cally! She ordered herself to stop being so teen-ager-with-a-crush.

She realized, in terms of the job, she didn't have any idea what was best for her. It was all too heady, like trying to make a decision when you were full of champagne.

"I need to go home," she said. "I have a place, beside the Falls, where I like to sit when I have a decision to make. It's free of distractions. No phones, no computers." Of course, she didn't have those things now, but she did have the big-gest distraction of all: Jamie.

"The right answer always comes when I'm there."

"I envy you having a place like that."

"You could come one day, and see it." What was she doing? Trying to keep him in her life, even if she said no to the job? Trying to see what they would have left if they did not have this fabulous backdrop behind them?

"I could," he said, and she scanned his face. Was he placating her? Being polite? Or would he really like to see Timber Falls? She felt as if she would genuinely like to see him on her home ground. It would help her know if the strength of her feelings for him were real.

But it was complicated, because if he did meet her parents, if he did ever come to Timber Falls to see her, her mom and dad would jump to the conclusion it was serious. Knowing her parents, they would start picking names for grandchildren, and sharing them with him!

She'd known the man two days. Yes, she had to go home and get her head on straight. There would be no making a rational decision under these present circumstances.

So she might as well just enjoy the experience while it lasted!

When they got in, it was late, and yet Jessica could not help but notice that he was as reluctant to say good-night as she was.

They cleaned up the kitchen together, and then went into his living room. He put on music, and then patted the couch beside him.

"So little time left," he said. With relief? Or regret? Or some combination of both? "Tell me everything there is to know about you."

She laughed. "I wouldn't know where to start. And it's not interesting."

"Start at the first day of school, when you told me you met your guy. And let me decide if it's interesting."

And so she found herself telling him about growing up in a small town, surrounded by people who knew you and were related to you. She told him about swimming in mountain lakes, and decorating the trees in their teachers' yards with toilet paper rolls, and picking huckleberries on hot summer days, riding their horses down tree-shaded trails.

She told him of her and Devon, always together, best friends.

"It was such a perfect life," she said, and heard the wistfulness in her own voice. "And then when he died, there was an awareness I had never had before. That life was not safe, that everything you loved could be taken from you in a blink.

"The bookstore was my grandmother's. I had never considered owning her bookstore, though I had always worked there. But then she wanted to retire, and Devon had died and it seemed like a natural choice."

"A way to make your world safe again. Predictable."

Trust him to see that, so quickly, and so completely.

"Yes," she said, with tears forming in her eyes. "Yes, I've played it very safe ever since Devon died. And it seems every time I've tried to step away from that safety net, all my fears about life are proven entirely correct."

"Tell me about that."

"I've hinted about my online dating disaster. The truth was, I didn't really feel ready to meet anyone. I think it was a reaction to everyone in town suggesting it was time to get over it. One of the joys of small towns is that everyone knows your business, and weighs in on everything about your life, usually without an invitation."

"So, you met a guy online, which takes the pressure off. Shows people you're getting on with things, without really changing anything."

"Quit being so astute! Anyway, it was a catastrophe. I finally decided to meet him. At the Annual Ascot Music Festival. Have you heard of it?

"Oh, yeah."

Of course he would have heard of it! He was cosmopolitan.

"Well, I hadn't. But I decided to meet him. It

was all on the up-and-up. I paid my own way, and insisted on my own room."

"He let you? Pay your own way?"

"I insisted!"

"Okay," he said in a tone that let her know that's not how it would have happened with him.

"And anyway, I was glad I did, because then I didn't owe him anything. And in person, he was an absolute jerk. Full of himself and self-centered. There was a lady at the music festival who had lost her dog and was hurt, and he acted as if he was more important than that. As if it was a big inconvenience to him. I made a decision, on the spot, to not let it go any further with him."

"Good for you. So then you came home and licked your wounds until now?"

"Yes."

"A perfect excuse to play it safe some more?" he suggested, his tone gentle.

She wasn't used to this, someone *seeing* her so clearly.

"Well, that might be true, but I did meet two women who have become lifelong friends."

"Uh-huh."

"More safety?" she guessed from his tone.

He lifted a shoulder at her.

"Anyway, there is nothing wrong with playing it safe. Look at this time! I took another chance, and another catastrophe."

"Really?" he said, softly. "I would think this is about the furthest thing from a catastrophe that I could imagine."

He was right. He was 100 percent right. She was living an absolute dream.

"Maybe the message from life," he suggested, "is that bad things happen. They happen to all of us. And we survive. Sometimes, if we look closely there can be a gift hidden in our worst moments."

She looked deeply at him, and his eyes so full of wisdom, and felt herself falling deeper. Tumbling toward him and what he offered.

A world that rewarded bravery.

A world where she could trust someone to be honest with her.

She could feel herself leaning toward him, leaning toward the adventure. And he leaned toward her, too.

Their lips met. Two souls who knew each other, who had known each other since the beginning of time and would know each other until the end.

He tasted of what he was: strength and calm.

But that strength, that she loved, and that was so obvious about him, was also what made him pull away from her.

"You know we can't," he said softly.

"If I don't take the job, can we?"

He laughed softly. "Now there's as poor a reason for making a career decision as I've ever heard."

He got up from her reluctantly. He stood over her for a moment, then reached down and cupped her cheek in his hand. He gazed at her face as though he were trying to memorize it. And then, he bent, placed one more gentle kiss on her lips, turned and went down the hall, into his bedroom. The door clicked shut with a kind of firm finality.

CHAPTER EIGHT

IT WAS JESSICA'S last day in NYC, and already it was showing every sign of being perfect. To her surprise, after putting her off last night, Jamie had joined her this morning.

From the moment he had introduced her to Patience and Fortitude, the marble lions that guarded the main entrance to the New York Public Library, Jessica had been enchanted. They had joined a tour, just leaving. Jessica had been enraptured with every square inch of that iconic building,

And the truth was, not just with the building.

It was having another incredibly memorable experience with Jamie at her side. It was remembering his lips, the taste of them, it was the potential, in the air between them for *more*.

It was her last day here. Jessica could already feel a sense of loss—and something else.

She was going to say yes. She was going to say yes to this incredible opportunity that was being offered her. She was going to say yes to the adventure. Maybe not forever. She distrusted forever.

But what would the harm be in trying it?

And did the sizzle between her and Jamie have anything to do with her saying yes?

If anything, she saw it as a complication. He really was going to be her boss. He probably wasn't going to be available to act as her tour guide, to eat pizza with, to take her to shows, to cook homemade meals for, to go on carriage rides through Central Park.

But he would be part of her life.

And she wanted that. She wanted to know him better. She could see the fabric of their lives weaving together. Perhaps fate had even ordained this. Even the theft, forcing them closer together, destiny having its way with them...

She stopped suddenly.

She was making plans for her whole life without checking in with a single soul. She had not checked in since she got here. She had not looked at any of her social media accounts and, apart from that first phone call to her parents, she had not talked to anyone.

Not being connected had felt freeing, and amazingly so.

But now, she couldn't help but wonder if she was living in a bubble. Jamie Gilbert-Cooper was just the kind of guy who could make a woman erase every other thing from her reality.

She needed to check in with her real life. She needed to ground herself. And just as she was recognizing that, she saw one of the library workstations—with a computer—come available.

Jamie had been emailing her pictures of their excursions. She could pick them up, and make a few posts. She could message with her mom and dad, and Daisy and Aubrey.

She suddenly recognized how momentous a turn in the road she had come to. She *needed* the input of those closest to her. She needed to know she had not given herself over to a fantasy, a fairy tale.

"I should use one of those computers," she said. "Can you give me half an hour?"

"Of course. I'm not sure if you have to be a member, but I can sign you in if you do."

Jessica signed in under Jamie's library account, and picked up the photos he had been emailing her. She could feel the delight unfolding in her as she looked at each of them. It confirmed her decision. She would take the job. She would move here. She would embrace the unknown.

I will let myself finish what I have started, which is falling in love with Jamie Gilbert-Cooper.

But that was the problem, wasn't it? Was she basing her decision on any of the right things?

She opened the message app on her favorite social media account. She sent her mother a picture of her with the lions in the background and a quick note saying she had seen *Phantom of the Opera* and been to the Russian Tea Room.

It was as if her mother had been waiting—which she probably had, Jessica realized guiltily.

Her mother wrote back.

So exciting. What's the job like? What are your thoughts?

Jessica replied that she was undecided and, after a little more conversation with her mother, reviewed some of her other social media accounts.

Jessica saw she had messages from both Daisy

and Aubrey, but before she could open them, Aubrey saw she was online and popped up on chat.

How is it going? Why haven't we heard from you?

Awful incident at the airport. All my luggage, my computer and phone stolen. Haven't posted anything about it, as I don't want Mom and Dad to worry. I'm using the computer at the New York Public Library right now. So much to tell you!

And Daisy and I to tell you!! We have both been given the most extraordinary gifts. Daisy got a house in Italy.

What?

Yes! And I've been given the funds to have the most grand adventure of my entire life. I can afford to circle the globe, travel, have adventures. I feel as if I've won a lottery!

I don't really understand.

We don't either. We've been waiting for you to check in, because we think your job offer is related, too.

In what way?

Well, doesn't it seem just a little too coincidental that all three of us are being given these opportunities? Not just gifts, really, but life-changing chances?

Jessica could feel something in her going cold.

From who?

But then, she knew. There was only one thread connecting the three of them. That little old lady and her dog that they had helped in Copenhagen. The three of them had talked about that before: how Viv had said she wanted to keep in touch, but though Aubrey, Daisy and Jessica had, Viv had not. While she had accepted their friend and contact requests, her social media accounts had never been used and she had never responded to messages or inquiries after her health.

Daisy and I think she might be Vivian Ascot.

I don't think I recognize that name.

Yes, you do. Ascot Corporation. They were the big sponsors of the music festival. It's one of the biggest corps in the world. They're into everything from ducks to doughnuts. Didn't you say your job interview was with Jensen, Henry and Ascot?

Aubrey had underlined Ascot to make her point. Jessica stared at the screen and felt as if the bottom was falling out of her world. It was a worse shock than having her things stolen. She'd been tricked. Deceived.

Oh, no doubt Viv—if this was Viv behind all this—thought she was doing a good deed, repaying some perceived debt or act of kindness.

But it meant that Jessica hadn't been chosen for this job because of her qualifications, or her know-how.

She felt a fool. How could she have believed, even for one second, that the owner of a miniscule bookstore in a town no one had ever heard of, which did not even deserve its own dot on the map, had come to the attention of an international firm like JHA?

No wonder she had been picked off at the airport! She might as well have had "easy mark" tattooed across her forehead.

And he was part of it! Jamie was part of it.

She'd planned to abandon her parents. And her bookstore. And her community. On the power of a kiss! She was deeply ashamed of herself.

And she was shocked by her lack of discernment. Last night, she had felt as if she could trust this man almost more than anyone else she had ever met! She wasn't just so naive they could pick her off at the airport, she was an immature fool.

I've just about got interim travel documents in place, so I'll be heading home soon. I'll call you and Daisy when I get there.

We haven't talked about your job yet! Or NYC.

Her job. Jessica felt unnaturally irritated that Aubrey hadn't picked up on it. It was a joke. A sham. There was no job. It was a creation of some little old lady with way too much time on her hands and way too much money. You didn't shape people's lives as if they were children's modeling clay just waiting to be molded!

She logged off the computer, resisting a temptation to try a seedy site while she was signed in under Jamie's name. What would happen? Alarms go off? An investigation into him? His reputation smirched? It would be a stupid, childish, "take that" gesture.

As she got up from the computer, she saw him coming toward her.

He was every bit as glorious as the first time she had laid eyes on him. It could make a woman weak when she desperately needed to be strong.

"What's wrong?" he said, as he came up to her. He took her shoulders in his hands. "Jessica? What's happened? Did you get bad news from home?"

"Bad news," she said, shaking out from under his hands, "but not from home."

She turned away from him and went out the main exit, past Patience and Fortitude, the magic of meeting them dissipated.

The magic of this city dissipated.

Suddenly it didn't seem energetic and vibrant and as if she could never get enough.

It felt dirty and noisy and crowded and she just wanted to go home.

"Jessica—" he put his hand on her shoulder and she spun around. "What's happened?"

His face, the genuine concern that darkened his eyes, made her feel as if she could be made of steel, and still melt. She had to be strong!

She drew in a sharp breath and jerked out from under his hand.

"Does the name Vivian Ascot mean anything to you?"

"You know Ascot is part of our company name," he said, his tone guarded.

"I did know that. What I didn't know was that a little old lady that I told you about last night—the one I helped at the music festival in Copenhagen—had that name. I knew her only as Viv. But you know her, don't you?"

"Not really. She's mostly a silent partner. I met her once."

"The whole thing—the whole job offer—is some pathetic act of charity, isn't it?"

"No! Not as far as I know."

"What I want to know is what is your part in all of this?"

"Look, I admit, at first I thought the old gal was off her rocker, recommending you for a job."

Off her rocker.

"Was there a job? Or did she create one?"

His look of discomfort was all the answer she needed. "What was your part in it?" she asked again. Jessica could hear something dangerous in her voice. And so could he.

He hemmed uncomfortably.

"Be honest with me," she said, of the man that just last night she had thought was one of the most honest she had ever met. "If you are capable of it."

He flinched from that. "Okay. I wasn't sure why she picked me to meet you. I admit I thought it was a punishment."

"Meeting me was a punishment?" she asked. Her voice was shrill enough that a few heads turned toward them.

"That came out wrong."

"Did it, now?"

"I crossed swords with her. I didn't like her name for the music festival in Copenhagen. I don't even remember it now."

"Carlene to Celine and Everything In Between."

"That's it," he said with a wince. "Really, it was so trivial I thought she'd forgotten it. But then when I got the order I was supposed to personally meet your plane and look after you when you got here, I thought it was payback time."

"So, Miss Ascot got me here on a false pretense, and I was some kind of revenge to you against some slight against her?"

"That's what I thought. But I was wrong, Jessica. Really wrong. When I saw you meet our clients, I realized she knew what she was doing. You have something. You—"

"Oh, spare me. How would I know you were telling the truth?"

He looked like she had slapped him, and she was glad!

"Everything we did was about looking after me, wasn't it? From the Russian Tea Room to *The Phantom of the Opera*—"

"No, it wasn't," he told her tightly.

She barely heard him. "Your grand obligation, your need to win back Viv after a fall from favor. You should be very pleased with yourself. I actually thought you were enjoying spending time with me. Last night? I thought I could trust you to tell me how it really is. Isn't that a laugh?"

"Jessica—"

But she was beyond listening to him. "Even the clothes were part of the grand lie, weren't they? Those clothes from Hennessey's. How much were they really worth?"

He was silent.

"They were worth a fortune, weren't they? You had Meredith make up a bill that coincided with what the insurance company said they would give me."

"It was just making you so happy. I wanted—"

"Lies do not make people happy!" she said. "I'm an adult. Do you get that? I don't need you, or anyone else, to look after me, to decide the course of my life for me."

His mouth opened to protest and then closed again.

"When you get back to your apartment," she told him, "you can box all those clothes up and take them back. Some things still have the tags on. Anything I wore can go to Goodwill. But I'll pay for it all. I'll send you the e-transfer as soon as I get home. I don't want it anymore."

"Look, we're both going back to the apartment, and we're talking this thing through."

"Again, you're going to make all the decisions, as if I'm a child who needs your guidance? What exactly is the point of talking it through?" She cocked her head at him. "You think I'm gullible, don't you?"

"That's not how I would put it."

"And that's not a no. I bet you've found this all quite hilarious—small-town girl's infatuation with super suave you!"

He cocked his head at her. He frowned. "Infatuation?" he asked softly.

And then she realized she had said way too much, and revealed way too much. Unable to bear one more moment, afraid her anger was going to turn to tears, she turned and ducked into the crowd.

"Jessica!"

But she spotted the rarest thing you could ever see in New York City—an empty cab—idling at the curb, waiting for a customer.

She jumped in and closed the door.

"Where to?"

She could see Jamie racing toward them. Where to? "Take me to the Canadian Consulate office," she said, and the cab pulled away, leaving Jamie standing there. She was pleased to see the faint look of panic on his face.

His charge had escaped him.

She hoped he would have fun explaining that to Vivian Ascot!

As the cab squeezed out into traffic, she turned and looked at Jamie one more time. And an awful truth nudged her.

Was this really about Vivian Ascot?

Or was this a convenient excuse to run? To not face her deepest fear.

Which is? she asked herself. No answer came.

Jamie watched helplessly as the cab pulled away. He felt afraid for her. It was a big city and she had few skills for navigating it.

He saw another cab coming, lifted his arm to flag it, and then, slowly put it down and turned away.

It was more of the same, it was more of the very same thing she was accusing him of: not treating her like an adult, taking charge, protecting her. As much as it bugged him, he had to trust her to find her own way.

He went to work and tried to clear Jessica from his mind. It was not that easy. Her parting words about *infatuation* clawed at his insides. She cared about him. She had trusted him. And he had blown it. He had blown it, even though he cared about her, too.

Which was just proof he was unsuited for the whole serious relationship thing. He didn't have a clue how to navigate any situation that required any depth. Jessica required depth.

Why was he even thinking about her in terms of a serious relationship?

He cared about her, yes, but he barely knew her. They barely knew each other. And yet, even as Jamie tried to convince himself of that, he sensed the lie.

They knew each other. There had been a serious, serious connection between them. In that light, it was good that she was gone. No, more than good. It was *great.* She was the kind of woman who could make even a hedonistic self-centered guy like him put his life under the microscope. Look hard at it. Find it—and himself—lacking.

She was the kind of woman that could make a man long for something more, feel his whole life was a desert of shallowness and meaninglessness, and that she held an answer, she could guide him to the oasis.

Jessica Winton could do that after two days! He was *glad* she was gone.

But when he entered his apartment after work, it seemed dark and lifeless and empty. He found himself in the bedroom she had used.

Her scent was in the air again—lavender. It made him ache, which made him feel furious with himself. That fury propelled him to the closet. He would do exactly as she instructed. She wanted to be an adult? She wanted to be in charge? Fine, he'd send all that stuff to Goodwill, just as she requested. He'd do it right now—he'd banish her from his space and from his heart.

He opened the door and saw *that* dress, the cocktail dress, in wisps of blue so insubstantial the dress might have been constructed of fog. It was the dress that she had worn to *Phantom of the Opera* and memory flooded him.

Memories of every single moment they had shared crowded around him. He went into the closet and buried his nose in the fabric.

He thought about how much she had loved that dress. Most women would have wanted it, would have taken it, especially if they were mad. All the women he'd ever met kept his gifts when it was over. But she wanted to give them away?

Somehow he knew, despite her ability to think of someone else, even when she was in distress, he knew he would not be sending that dress, or anything else of hers, to Goodwill.

He also knew she was the kind of woman who would require him—any man she was with—to be a better man.

"Not up for that," he said out loud, as if somehow that would make it true, as if it would take away the unexpected longing to be the kind of man worthy of a woman like Jessica.

He told himself, again, he was glad she was gone.

The words rang as hollow as a tree that had had its insides burned clean out by a lightning strike.

CHAPTER NINE

"JESSICA, YOUR FATHER and I have to talk to you. Can we come over?"

Jessica sighed. This was the problem with living in a little cottage in your parents' back-yard. Of course they could come over, they were steps away. She couldn't even pretend she wasn't home. Her mother's kitchen window looked right at her house. They would have known the second she returned from the bookstore today.

Funny how since she'd returned from New York, she was so aware of the "problems" in her life. Town too stifling, parents too close, house too small, bookstore not challenging. Her trip to New York had triggered a deep sense of dissatisfaction in her. Which explained why she had been avoiding her parents. It made her feel guilty that she suddenly yearned for things she had never yearned for before.

Including the taste of a certain man's lips.

But still, all those "problems" seemed like

they might only be distractions from the real issue. And yet, she recoiled from the question that pressed at the edges of her mind every time she lay down to go to sleep: What was the *real* reason she had run away from Jamie?

If she craved the taste of his lips, if she wanted him in her life, why hadn't she stayed and talked to him? Heard his side of things? At least given whatever was happening between them an opportunity to grow? Should she call him? Should she apologize?

Before she could go too far down that road, there was a knock on the door. Jessica realized she should have offered to go over to their place. Her small space was something it had never been before—a disaster! Since her return, looking after her own space seemed like too much of an effort.

She opened the door and her mother and father filed in, looking very solemn, casting worried glances at her and the state of her house, on the way to her kitchen table.

"Jessica," her mother said, without preamble, "you've been home a week. Your father and I can't help but notice you seem depressed."

Depressed? Did it go that far? She looked

around her tiny home: empty ice cream buckets on the counter, dishes piled in the sink, clothes on the floor. Good grief! This was not her.

"We know you told us you were robbed in New York. We were wondering about post-traumatic stress. Maybe some counseling—"

Jessica bit her lip. It was the first time she had felt like laughing since she got home. "Mom, I'm okay. I don't have PTSD. Honestly, the robbery…" she hesitated. What could she say? Led to the best experience of her entire life? "… just didn't affect me that much."

If that was true, if it had led to the best experience of her life, why had she been so quick to run, to slam the door shut behind her?

"But something has!" her mother wailed. "Your father and I have talked about it. Another possibility we thought of was that you fell in love with New York, didn't you?"

For a heart-stopping moment, Jessica heard *you fell in love in New York, didn't you?*

She didn't say anything, so her mother rushed on.

"If that's what's bothering you—if you want to go there—we support you 100 percent. We would miss you dreadfully, of course, but we are still young people, quite capable of looking after ourselves. We're not doddering old fools, even if we can't run our phones. Or the TV set."

"Don't forget the tablets," her father added, pleased to be of help.

Her mother shot him a look.

Jessica saw, between them, in that look of exasperated affection, everything she had always wanted. Comfort, companionship, love that had survived many tests and challenges, a deep *knowing* of another human being.

Her parents, she knew, from their stories, had been just like Jessica and Devon: lifelong companions, soul mates who had grown up next door to each other.

But in New York, Jessica had glimpsed something far more terrifying than their steady love, something that burned brighter and hotter.

There was that fear again, flitting around the edges of her mind. She shoved it away.

"What your mother is trying to say is that we would never want you to put off an opportunity out of a sense of obligation to us."

"Yes, that is exactly what I wanted to say. Just think! We could visit you in NYC. It's on my bucket list."

They were both looking at her so hopefully, wanting so desperately to fix anything that was wrong in her world.

Jessica could feel tears forming in her eyes. Her parents were setting her free, giving her their blessing. But in her heart, she knew it wasn't a sense of obligation to her parents holding her back.

That was just one of her many excuses.

"Thank you," she told them softly.

Her father took that as a signal to leap up from his chair and get away from a conversation that was not about an old car, so therefore was uncomfortable.

"I have to work on that lock thing," he said, and hauled his phone out of his pocket. "Look, Jessica, I can lock the doors of the house from here. I'm trying to hook up the bookstore for you, but—"

Her mother gave him a nudge and a warning look.

"But I can do it myself!" he said. "No need for you to help, Jessica. At all."

After they left, she looked at the clock. There was time, before dark, to go to the Falls. She had told Jamie that she always went there when she needed an answer, but she had been making the hike almost daily, and still no answers came.

New York had shown her an uncomfortable truth. Jessica had outgrown her hometown. Now what? Obviously, New York had not worked out, but should she be actively seeking out other opportunities? Thinking of selling her bookstore? Moving on?

She might have normally sounded out these ideas on Aubrey and Daisy. She had come to trust their judgment deeply. They were definitely her "go-to" when she needed to share a confidence.

But this time, they were in a tizzy of excitement over the shocking gifts they had been given.

Neither of them would entertain the notion that their gifts—Daisy, a villa in Italy, and Aubrey, funds to go on a grand adventure—were very different than hers. Neither of their gifts was directed at their professional competency. While their gifts seemed only to reflect the generosity of the giver, seemed to be only about embracing *fun*, Jessica felt the weight of a judgment in the gift of a job opportunity, as if Viv had sniffed out a failure, as if the opportunity she had directed toward Jessica was based in pity.

Aubrey had scoffed at the idea, and Daisy had been silent when Jessica had said it, which Jessica assumed was disagreement. So, she had gone quiet online, feeling, not quite betrayed by her two friends, but not understood, either.

Suddenly, she had the feeling. *They knew.*

Aubrey and Daisy knew that Jessica's feelings of upheaval may have been precipitated by the unexpected job offer, but they had not been caused by it.

Indeed, it might have all brought her to this place she most needed to be.

Facing the fear that was at the core of her being, and that directed every single other thing in her life.

Jamie swatted at a mosquito. He felt as if he had been on the longest journey of his life, and it had brought him to the very edges of the earth.

Timber Falls was not an easy place to reach. It had taken nearly two days to get here, including the flight and renting a car from the nearest airport. After driving through a wilderness of towering trees and soaring mountains—country so endless and magnificent it made a man feel small and lost—his GPS had finally delivered him to Timber Falls.

It was a town out of a postcard: against a backdrop of ragged-edged mountains and deep green forests, was a wide valley that held neat and tidy streets, lined with pastel-painted cottages and Victorian houses in historical colors. There were shady porches, with swings on them, fenced yards with patches of lush green grass that begged for bare toes to wiggle in it. He caught glimpses of garden plots with neat rows of furry green growth poking up through rich black soil. Everywhere were lilac trees, in full blooms of white, lavender, deep purple. The summer air was perfumed with their scent.

He passed two churches, small boxes of buildings with soaring spires, and a water park where children squealed as they squirted each other with cannon-like guns and as a bucket on a post filled and then spilled over on top of them. The elementary school and the high school shared grounds, the soccer fields and baseball diamonds empty, the swings in the play yard deserted for the summer.

The outlying neighborhoods gave way to a

quaint main street, baskets overflowing with colorful petunias hanging from old-fashioned streetlight standards. At two stories, the tallest buildings were the town hall, and the Royal Bank.

It was all exactly as Jamie had pictured the town Jessica would come from.

He drove slowly, passing the hardware store, a restaurant, a bakery, a hair salon. And there it was. Sandwiched in between a false-fronted ice cream store and a sandstone art gallery was a narrow old house that had been converted into a bookstore.

The plate glass window had a graphic in Baskerville Old Face that declared it was Jessica's store, The Book and Cranny.

Jamie could feel his heart begin to beat faster in anticipation of seeing her again. How would she react? Surely she would not slam a door in his face when she knew how hard it was to get to this place?

He was here on official business, but if that was completely true, his heart would not be beating nearly out of his chest at the thought of seeing her.

He got out of his car and was blasted by early-summer heat. He hurried across the sidewalk and opened the door of her store.

A bell rang when the door opened. The store should have felt dark after the bright sunlight of outside, but it didn't. He had expected he might feel closed in by shelves of books, but instead the space felt open, cheery, light-filled and wonderfully cool.

He could see Jessica's touch everywhere: in the beautiful little nook that the store had probably taken its name from, which was filled with colorful pillows, in the sunflower-yellow wall hung with framed posters for favorite children's books: *Where the Wild Things Are, Love You Forever, Goodnight Moon.*

A well-loved copy of *Are You My Mother?* was open on its spine on one of the pillows. He scanned the space and saw only four people: a mother with two children, and a middle-aged man flicking through the newspaper selection.

No Jessica. In fact, there was no evidence that anyone was employed here. He walked around and looked at hand-lettered signs on the walls.

We can book you without an arrest.
Odds are we're your favorite bookie.

Caught you read-handed.
We're all about buy the book.

Then a door opened, and he held his breath, then let it go again when an elderly woman came out from an office area and set some books on the service counter. He craned his neck to see into the office, but she frowned at him and closed the door.

He walked over to the counter. "I'm looking for Jessica Winton."

The woman lowered half-glasses to the tip of her nose and regarded him silently for a long moment. "She's not here. She left early. She's been leaving quite early every day since she came back from New York City."

She said this in a faintly accusing tone, as if she could read where he came from, from a mile away. As if Jessica had returned to them changed, and she saw that as his fault. Had she returned changed?

Reading way too much into it, he told himself sternly. He was here on business. He couldn't very well ask where she lived, could he? Or maybe he could, since it felt like the pretense of business, not that he could afford any more pretense around Jessica!

"When will she be back?"

"Tomorrow morning."

Did he look as deflated as he felt? Because the woman's expression inexplicably softened, and she pushed her glasses back up on her nose.

"You could try the Falls," she said. "I've seen her going up that way several times."

Small towns, where everyone *knew* what everyone else was doing and weren't afraid to share it, either. What if a stranger was seeking Jessica for nefarious purposes? He wanted to say something to the woman about revealing her boss's whereabouts, but Jamie reminded himself, as he exited the store back into the heat, that Jessica had not appreciated his feeling protective of her.

The Falls. She had told him that was where she went for answers. What answer did she seek since she had returned to this place?

Swatting at mosquitos, it occurred to Jamie that he was in her home territory this time. It might be that he was the one needing protection. Weren't there bears around here? His shoes didn't seem particularly well suited to this activity either. How far were the Falls?

He heard them before he saw them, a roar in the distance that grew louder and louder until he could see mist in the air. He came around a final twist in the pathway and stopped short.

Jessica was sitting on a large, flat rock, facing the Falls. Her eyes were closed and her face was lifted to the mist that fell around her. Her knees were drawn up to her and her arms were wrapped around them. She had on a sleeveless white tank top, belted khaki shorts and sturdy hiking boots. In the time she had been back here, her skin had become sun-kissed and was the warm golden brown of a loaf of bread fresh from the oven. Her hair was in a braid that hung over one shoulder.

She did not look like the same woman as he had spent time with in New York: she seemed more natural, completely at home with herself, more stunningly beautiful, if that was possible.

She must have sensed she was no longer alone, because she dropped her head, opened her eyes and turned to look at him.

For one moment, in her eyes, he saw surprise, followed by unbridled joy.

He was aware a man could live for such a look from a woman.

But then the look was gone, so quickly he wondered if it was a trick of light and mist, an illusion created by the rainbows that danced in the air around her.

"Hello, Jessica," he said, having to raise his voice to be heard over the thunder of the Falls.

She slid off the rock, brushed off the seat of her shorts and faced him, her arms crossed over her chest.

"What are you doing here?" she demanded, the look a man could live for gone completely from her beautiful face.

Jessica could not take her eyes off Jamie. He was out of his element, and impossibly it made him even more gorgeous! That beautifully cut suit, the jacket hooked over his shoulder with his thumb, made him look like a model ready for a photo shoot in a rugged location. His hair was falling sexily over one eye, and he looked as confident as he had on the streets of New York.

She had been coming here for answers since her return from the big city but the Falls had been stubbornly silent. How could she have known him for such a short period of time, and her heart whispered *beloved* when she saw him?

When Jamie had come out of the mist, he had seemed as if he could be her answer.

But wasn't he the kind of man who a lot of women probably thought was their answer? By his own admission his very own sister said he had made capturing hearts a game. Besides, here was the truth: people needed to provide their own answers!

She had to steel herself against that abundance of charm and confidence. She had to steel herself against the cry of her own heart.

"What are you doing here?" she asked him again.

"I was sent here. To talk to you."

Sent here. She was still some kind of assignment. "Oh," she said, and tossed her braid over her shoulder, "*punishment*. You let the charity case get away."

His expression darkened. "It was never like that. Vivian Ascot has amazing instincts. She hasn't gotten to where she is in business on her inheritance alone, believe me. You have something she wants, and I've been sent to get it."

Jessica actually felt disappointed. He was here for business, not because he had missed her. Not because he had thought of her every day. Not because those thoughts had crowded out all else and filled him with an insane sense of longing. Not because his life had suddenly felt as it was lacking and as if he needed to change everything.

"What does she want?" Jessica had tried to get in touch with Vivian since she and Daisy and Aubrey had figured out that was who their benefactress was. They all had. But as Daisy had put it, *"You'd think she was the Queen."*

Her security was impenetrable. They couldn't even tell if Vivian knew about their multiple social media attempts to reach her, or if they had all been relegated to the spam pile.

"She—we, JHA—want to see, firsthand, how you are making that bookstore such a phenomenal success. If you won't come to work for us, we'll come to you. We're hoping you'll agree to let us use your bookstore as a model. We'd compensate you, naturally."

The only part that interested her was the *"we."* JHA. Not *me*. Not *I*.

"It's unnecessary to compensate me," Jessica said stiffly. She also realized she was slightly miffed that he wasn't here to beg her to change her mind. "And it was unnecessary to come here.

I could have sent you any information that you needed."

"You could have," he agreed.

"But that wouldn't have been a punishment, then, would it?"

"This isn't a punishment. I asked to come. I wanted to see you in your own environment."

She studied his face, and found she could not meet the steadiness of his gaze. She could feel her heart spinning crazily. He was here because he wanted to be. A woman not as determined to find her own way as Jessica was could read way too much into that.

She, accidentally, looked at his lips. She remembered the taste of them and felt dizzy with longing, weak with a need to throw herself at him, feel his arms come around her, cover his face with tiny kisses, tangle her hands in the silky gray of his hair.

Instead, she brushed by him and headed back down the trail, fast.

"Those shoes are ridiculous for a hike in the mountains," she called to him over her shoulder.

"Believe me, I already figured that out."

"You want to see how my bookstore works?

You want to use it as a model? Fine. How long are you here for?"

"I thought I'd stay the whole day tomorrow, and leave the following morning," he said, his tone cautious.

"Perfect. You can get some firsthand experience with the *model*—and not the kind of model I assume you're used to, either."

"What kind would that be?"

"Long-legged, photogenic." She noticed he did not deny it. Of course he was the type that dated models! No surprise there. "Story time is tomorrow at ten. You can lead it."

"I'm not that good with kids."

"You have a nephew."

"At a distance!"

"That's just sad."

"Look, Jessica, I'm trying to tell you I'm not a kid person."

Maybe what he was really trying to tell her was that he was not husband material. Good grief! Was she looking at him like he was husband material?

"You read them a story. You don't have to be good with them."

"How old are they?"

"Three to five."

He looked nonplussed. "Don't you need a criminal record check, or something? To work with kids?"

"Working with them is overstating it. Don't worry, their mothers will be there."

Ogling the super cute guy from the big city who had I date models *written all over him.*

"Is there a gang of them?"

"We don't have gangs in Timber Falls," she told him, straight-faced. "Expect five or six kids."

Then, knowing in those shoes he could never catch her, she started to jog down the trail.

"Are there bears out here?" he called after her.

"Yes! And cougars."

"Cougars?" he said, and inserted a theatrical hopeful note into his voice.

"Not that kind, you pervert."

"That's right! A pervert. I should not be asked to work with children."

She wanted to be indifferent to him, but it was impossible. "Also, the odd wolf. Definitely coyotes."

"You'll be sorry if I get eaten, Jessica Winton! Who will lead story time then?"

She didn't turn back to him. She didn't want to let him see her smiling. She didn't want him to know just how easily she was charmed by him.

"Are you going to at least offer to take me out for dinner?" he called. "I did that for you."

"You thought of it as a punishment," she reminded him.

"You can think of it the same way."

Somehow, she could not. "I have plans for tonight." This was not exactly the truth, unless watching TV was considered a plan, but there was no sense him thinking she was just going to set her life aside since the big, important man from New York had arrived.

"Oh," he said. He sounded disappointed. Which was elating. He also sounded as if he had not even considered the possibility she might have a life here in Timber Falls. Which was insulting.

He made her life complicated without even trying, she thought grumpily.

"Go to Henry's for supper," she told him. "They have the best burger in town. And try the B and B on First Street. I bet they'll let you check in without ID."

"As they should. I'm a completely trustworthy person."

"Ha. Tell that to someone who wasn't offered a fake job by you."

"We need to talk about that. Obviously it—"

She realized he was engaging her, even though she had decided not to be engaged by him. "Tomorrow at ten," she interrupted him, and then broke into a jog down the familiar trail, literally leaving him in her dust.

That night, lying in her bed, sleepless, because she knew he was just down the street—probably had charmed the socks off all the local girls at Henry's tonight—she warned herself against feeling the way she did.

Alive. Tingling with the delight of having seen him again, the anticipation of spending the day with him tomorrow.

I am falling in love with him, she realized, shocked. It was like nothing she had ever felt before, certainly it was not the cozy-as-a-comfortable-shoe feeling she had had with Devon. It felt as if he was air, as if she needed him in order to breathe.

It seemed imperative that he not know this. She had already let it slip once that she was infatuated with him, but now she had to keep this secret to herself. He could never know she *regretted* not joining him for dinner.

In her head she made a complete schedule for him for the next day: he could lead story time, send emails to people she had tracked down books that she thought might interest them, play chess with the Court Chessters in the afternoon. Serendipitously, the Smitten Word met here tomorrow night, and he could be the guest speaker. She'd surprise him with that one.

Professionally, she'd throw everything she had at him in hopes it would keep the personal stuff at bay!

CHAPTER TEN

"I LOOKED UP books last night," Jamie told her in the morning. "*Truck in the Muck* is a current favorite of the under-five set. Have you got that?"

She slid him a look. He was dressed in jeans. That was a first. And a casual shirt, also a first. If he had any lingering trepidation at all about leading story time, it did not show now. He was, obviously, one of those highly adaptable people, who could rise to any challenge. He looked extraordinarily handsome—and at home—in her space.

He was also freshly shaven, and she could smell soap and aftershave, and it made her feel as if she had been drinking champagne. So much for keeping the personal stuff at bay!

She realized her bookstore—her safe place, her hidey-hole in all the world—was never going to feel the same.

But, in fact, it hadn't felt the same since she had returned from New York, anyway.

He also looked rested, not as though he had tossed and turned, and wondered endlessly what to wear today!

She had chosen casual, because really she did not have much to choose from. She longed for her dress with the poppies on it, but settled for a knit tank top and capris.

"I have it. You can't read that one, though. I bring in a dozen copies of the book we read at story time and today's story is *How Do You Do, Suzie Q?*"

"A dozen?"

"Some of the moms who come today will buy one for their own child, or to put away for a gift for later, or for the book bag."

"The book bag?"

"Not every family in Timber Falls can afford a brand-new book, and so I created the book bag. You buy one book for yourself, and another to donate that will find its way to a child who is in need."

"You know all the kids in town?"

"No, of course not. But as the idea caught on, people tell me, in confidence, which kids might be struggling a bit. They'll slip me a note, or call anonymously. So-and-so has a birthday coming up. Or not much under the Smith family tree this year for Christmas. Or John Doe has been invited to a birthday party, and his mom can't afford for him to bring a present."

He stared at her for a long time. "It's brilliant. But it's more."

She cocked her head at him.

"It's beautiful," he said softly. "It's like feeding the homeless, only better. Feeding minds and souls instead of bodies."

"You're making too much of it."

He looked at her steadily. "I don't think I am."

And she felt herself blushing as though he had said, not that her idea was beautiful, but that she was beautiful.

Because he was looking at her as if she was.

Thankfully, Phillip Morrison chose that moment to burst through the door, having freed himself of his mother. She would never tell Jamie—or anyone else—but his mom was a struggling single parent, and he was one of those kids who benefited from the book bag.

"Could we have *Truck in the Muck* today?" he asked, his voice loud, his eyes already darting around looking for things to wreck. Thankfully, she had done her best to Phillip-proof the kids section.

"A kindred spirit," Jamie said in an undertone to Jessica.

"Who are you?" Phillip demanded.

"You can call me Jamie. I'm reading the story today."

"I want *Truck in the Muck*," Phillip said, his voice getting shrill.

Jamie contemplated him for a moment, and then sank onto his heels so he could look the little boy right in the eye. "That's what I want, too," he said in a confidential tone. "Tell you what, if you will be my assistant for the first story, we will have two stories today."

Jamie had been here five minutes, and he was changing the rules. And yet, as she watched, a small light came on in Phillip, so starved for male attention, and the worst possible thing happened to Jessica.

"So this is my first time," Jamie said, rising to his feet, "what do we do?"

"Set out the pillows in a circle, here," Phillip said and raced off to the nook to grab pillows.

Jamie's eyes met hers, so filled with *knowing* about that little boy's life. As something hard around Phillip melted as Jamie and he set up the mom chairs, something hard around her heart melted, too. She could picture Jamie as a father. As each of those children came in, and appeared equally awestruck by their new story time leader, the vision intensified.

She should find something else to do.

But instead, entranced, she sat down with the moms in a circle of chairs behind the children.

He was a magnificent storyteller. He used different voices. He paused theatrically in all the right places, he lowered his eyebrows and raised them up. He controlled Phillip with firm ease that made Phillip putty in his hands.

"Oh, my goodness," Doris Anderson whispered to her. "I'm in love."

Even though Jessica shot Doris an exasperated look that reminded her she was a very happily married woman, secretly she knew exactly how Doris was feeling.

Exactly.

As promised, Jamie read the two stories, and then was swarmed by small people wanting hugs—Jessica had forgotten to tell him about that traditional ending for story time. He handled the unexpected assignment delightfully: uncomfortable, obviously, but soldiering through.

Normally, the mothers would grab a copy of the book that had been read today from the available stack, leave their children in the children's section and wander off to peruse a book for themselves.

Today, they surrounded Jamie, wanting information.

"Where are you from?"

"What are you doing here?"

"How long will you be here?"

He handled it all with grace and humor, and soon had those women around him laughing.

He's bad for sales, Jessica told herself crankily, even as she could not take her eyes off him.

He saw Phillip and his mother slipping out the door, and excused himself from the women he was talking to.

"Hey, buddy," he called.

Phillip turned around.

"This is for you." And he squatted down to eye level and presented him with the copy of *Truck in the Muck* that he was still holding.

Phillip stared at the book, and then threw himself into Jamie's arms with such strength he nearly bowled him over. Then he let go and ran out the door after his mother. Jamie's pristine shirt looked faintly grubby, and he didn't even brush at the stain the child had left on it. He looked down at it, with a funny smile on his face.

Jessica went to the till, where a line was forming. She had been wrong about Jamie being bad for sales. She sold eight children's books, three romance novels, a cookbook on dinners for two, and a dusty copy of the *Kama Sutra* that she had not been aware was in inventory. She was unable to meet Doris Anderson's eyes as she shoved it quickly in a bag.

The last person in line was Jamie, with his wallet out. He had another copy of *Truck in the Muck*. "Please ring up the one I gave him, and put this one in the book bag."

She did, as unable to meet his eyes as she had been when Doris Anderson bought the *Kama Sutra*, afraid of what he would see.

The awful, awful truth.

Falling. Falling. Falling.

Jamie found himself immersed in Jessica's world. It was a magical place. He quickly discovered people loved her bookstore. And why wouldn't they? It was warmly welcoming, a place to drop by for a chat with neighbors, a book browse, a quick look at the calendar of upcoming events that she posted and put a copy of in every single book bag that went out of there.

In the next month she was hosting two readings by authors, one "Summer Fun" theme night for teens and one for eight-to-twelve-year-olds. She had live music here every Thursday where she showcased local talent—and sold their CDs.

As well as hosting story time once a week, the bookstore hosted the chess club, whom he would be meeting this afternoon. She also provided evening meeting space for AA—now those people bought books; toastmasters—also book buyers; as well as a host of other local clubs, interest and support groups. She even brought in a fortune-teller twice a year.

She tracked people's buying habits and, without any pressure at all, she would show them a book she had discovered in their area of interest.

"Mr. Thompson, I came across this book on common fossils of the Rocky Mountains. Would you like to have a look?"

Or, "Pam, I found this book about elderly parents and Alzheimer's."

"Sheila, is Freddy still going through his dinosaur obsession? You might like this for him."

But none of this interest in her customers was the least bit mercenary—even though she sold a ton of books. She cared about these people. They were her friends, her neighbors, her relatives, people she had gone to school with, people her parents had gone to school with.

It was very evident to him as he shadowed Jessica through her day, that the people of her town loved her, and she loved them. Despite the fact she didn't sell any beverages or food—bad for the books—the bookstore was their gathering place, the heart and soul of their community.

She had managed, as far as he could see, to do the rarest of things. She mixed compassion, concern and genuine caring for people with her business. The Book and Cranny was not a repository of dusty tomes, but alive with energy and enthusiasm.

And it was Jessica at the heart of all that.

Jamie thought they could probably use her "model" all they wanted. They could package her procedures and document her successes and show her numbers in a glossy-covered report and distribute them to all their clients. But it would be missing the secret ingredient: Jessica Winton. Without her, would it be successful?

When he was with her, he couldn't help but remember how she had made him feel in New York: happy, engaged. Her company was imminently enjoyable. Could he revisit the possibility of her working for JHA?

But there was that other thing going on between them, too, just below the surface. Awareness of each other. A desire to touch—to brush hands, to graze shoulders. He tried to avoid looking at her lips, because every time he did he was nearly swamped by the memory of that taste of them.

So, how could they revisit her coming to work for JHA? He would be her boss. He didn't want to be her boss.

He wanted to be…

He was stunned by the word his mind filled in. *Lover.*

He wanted to be Jessica Winton's lover. He wanted her eyes to rest on him with hunger, and he wanted his touch to make her long for him.

He wanted to taste her all over. He wanted to possess her in every way it was possible for a man to possess a woman.

And he wanted her to possess him the same way.

"What?" Jessica asked him, turning back from the door to look at him. She had just ushered the last customer out, and put out the closed sign.

"Nothing." Too sharply, too quickly, too defensively.

"You were looking at me oddly."

"Was I?"

She gave him a quizzical look. "Never mind. We have time for a quick dinner, and then I have a group coming in tonight."

They left the store, and she locked the door behind her with a code. "Don't tell my dad," she told him with a laugh. "I'm supposed to be able to lock it with my phone. I don't have the heart to tell him it's not working right."

Her *dad*, he reminded himself. She was not the kind of girl a man could give himself over to having lascivious thoughts about!

But even with that stern reminder to himself, dinner was a torture of being aware of her. A hamburger! Not pheasant under glass, not Le

Bernardin, not anything special at all. But that little speck of mustard at the corner of her lip made awareness of her snap along his spine as though he was touching a live electrical wire.

This was what life would be if Jessica was in it: everything would become special, every moment lit from within. That was what she had done with that bookstore. She had infused it with her spirit and her sparkle and people were drawn to that.

As he was.

He had to get out of this place, and he had to get away from her. From the very beginning she had been an enchantress, waving a wand, and not changing the world, but changing the way he looked at it.

Back at the bookstore, she tried to use her phone to unlock the door, but it didn't work. She used her key and they went in.

Moments later, a woman arrived in a flurry of breathlessness.

"You must be our guest!" one of them—she reminded him, unfortunately, of Debbie of Gidgets Widgets fame.

"Your guest?" he asked.

"I'm Bailey Turnbull, president of the Smitten

Word. We're a group of women who meet to dis-
cuss our favorite topic—romance!"

His mouth fell open. He shot Jessica a look,
only to see she was smiling gleefully.

"That's a topic about which I know nothing,"
he said firmly.

"Nonsense. Have a seat here at the head of the
table. The rest of the girls will be here shortly."

There wasn't a girl among them, naturally.

"This is Jamie Gilbert-Cooper," Bailey introduced him. "He's here from New York City and
he's going to speak to us tonight on the topic of
romance in the city."

He shot Jessica another look. She was busy setting up a table by the counter with stacks of the
current Harlequin bestsellers, but her shoulders
were shaking with mirth.

He'd like to show her a thing or two about romance.

"I haven't really prepared anything," he said,
hoping for a short meeting.

"Oh, well just tell us what you would do if you
were wooing a girl," Bailey encouraged him.

He narrowed his eyes at Jessica. "I'd eat pizza
on a deck overlooking Central Park with her," he
said slowly. "I'd take her shopping. We'd watch

the kids float boats in the Conservatory Water in Central Park. I'd take her out for a nice dinner, at a restaurant in the Theater District called Le Bernardin. Then I'd take her to see *Phantom of the Opera* after. It has some scary surprises in it that practically guarantee a woman will be clutching your hand. We'd see some sights in New York, but there would definitely be a horse-drawn carriage ride."

"Oh," the women seemed to sigh in unison.

But Jessica had gone very still.

Possibly he and Jessica were both asking themselves the same question. It was supposed to have been a job interview.

But when he looked back over their time together, he didn't remember much about the business parts of it. Only the wonder of being with her. Was that wooing, then?

And why was he really here?

It occurred to him: *I can't stand the thought of a life without her in it.*

The ladies had lots of questions about New York City, his marital status, what he did for fun, what his ideal woman looked like—wasn't that her standing over there—and he did his best to be funny and engaging without revealing one personal thing about himself.

Thankfully, after the heat of the day, a terrible thunderstorm was brewing, and it knocked out the power. They were quite willing to wait and see if the power came back on, but Jessica insisted they go before the rain started.

Jessica had to usher the reluctant ladies out the door into the pitch-blackness of a town that did not have a single light burning in it except for the headlamps on cars.

When she closed the door, it made a loud clicking sound, and they both looked at it to see the dead bolt turning on its own.

"Good grief," she said, trying the handle, "I think we're locked in." She tried to open the dead bolt. It was stuck fast. Then she pulled out her phone and opened an app. She pushed something. Nothing happened. She handed him the phone. He pushed something. Nothing happened. She turned on the flashlight feature and they both looked at the door. There was no place to insert a key from the inside.

Now they were alone, locked in the bookstore. He could think of worse things.

"Good one," he said softly. "Me the guest speaker at a romance group."

"I just knew they would find you exotic and intriguing and delightful."

"You could have warned me."

"I could have," she agreed with an impish grin.

Lightning lit up the sky, and her face. Despite the grin, he could see something beneath it.

The hunger.

"Do you?" he asked her softly. "Find me exotic and intriguing and delightful?"

The world went dark again, but her voice came through the darkness.

"Yes," she said, hoarsely, "yes, I do."

And then he could not stop himself anymore. He reached through the pitch-blackness and his hand found the softness of her cheek. He heard her soft intake of breath, and he moved in closer to her.

His eyes adjusted to the darkness, and her face, illuminated by the odd flash of lightning, was possibly the most beautiful thing he had ever seen.

"That look you're giving me," he said gruffly, "it seems distinctly come-hither."

"Oh, it is," she assured him.

He could not resist her anymore. Not if he used all his logic. Not if he used all his strength. With the thunder rolling as the perfect background music to what was happening to his heart, he dropped his head over hers.

Tenderly, he took her lips. Outside the rain began to fall with drumming intensity.

It might have started as conquest, but it quickly became something on the opposite end of the spectrum. He felt the surrender in himself. He felt the surrender in her. He knew what was going to happen next.

It was all so wrong. She was not that kind of girl. A bookstore was not the ideal place to make love for the first time.

And yet, as he scooped her up in his arms, and took her back to that cushion-filled nook, nothing had ever felt so right.

Ever.

Not in his entire life. He laid her down in the pillows, and the lightning flashed as she held open her arms to him. He fell into them.

It felt as if every moment since he had met her had been leading to this one: finally, finally, he had her in his field of lavender, her sweet curves crushed beneath him, her scent enveloping them both, her lips tender and welcoming under his.

If he had expected reticence he had been wrong.

She was a woman who knew what she wanted. And she wanted him. A side of her he had not expected came forward: bold, adventurous, willing to explore.

And her lips explored him. They explored his face and his earlobes, her teeth nipping lightly. They explored his lips and then moved on again, down his shirt, her fingers finding his buttons and undoing them. Her hands closed around the sides of his ribs, and her lips moved down the column of his throat to his chest, grazing over one nipple and then the other.

A groan of the pure pain of wanting her escaped him. She stopped kissing him. Her eyes dark on his face, she reached up and opened the top button of her blouse.

"Jessica," he said hoarsely. "Are you—"

She nodded. "Sure. I'm sure."

And then he took her fingers away, and tenderly he undid the rest of the buttons. He flicked her blouse open and gazed at the wonder of her. Then he lowered his head and began the same exploration she had done on him: lips, ears, column of her throat, anointing her with the fiery brand of his kisses.

Something banged. He lifted his head. She drew his attention back to her. "The storm," she whispered.

But it was not the storm.

The bookstore door banged open with force, all the sounds of the storm—thunder and pounding rain—coming in with it.

Jamie pulled away from Jessica, blocking her body with his own. A flashlight beam caught him in the eye.

"Who the hell are you?" a man's voice asked.

"I think the question is who the hell are you?" he shot back, shoving himself up.

Behind him, he sensed Jessica frantically doing up buttons, doing something to the mess of her hair.

"Dad," she said, "this is Jamie Gilbert-Cooper."

Her dad, understandably, looked less than impressed.

Jamie did not know he was capable of the feeling that overcame him. Guilt. A terrible sense of remorse.

What did he think he was doing? Well, no that

wasn't the question. He knew exactly what he was doing.

What he had forgotten was *who* he was doing it with.

A young woman from a small town. Beloved to all. Adored by her family. Protected by her father.

Jamie had known all along that she was wholesome and traditional.

How could he have done what he just did?

She wasn't the kind of girl you had a tryst with. She wasn't the kind of girl a man had an entertaining dalliance with.

"Are you from New York?" her father asked, as Jamie quickly did up the buttons on his shirt.

"Yes."

"And are you the reason she's been so unhappy since she got back?"

Startled, Jamie looked at Jessica.

He could tell he was the reason.

Why had he come here? Why had he chased her down? It wasn't at all as he had said. Yes, Vivian Ascot had read the riot act to his boss, and yes, he had been sent to get Jessica's model for her bookstore.

But really? Anyone could have come.

But he'd insisted, like a man who had sipped an elixir that he couldn't get out of his head. That he couldn't get enough of.

She made him powerless.

But that was only an excuse—and a pathetic one at that—for not controlling himself. Her father had arrived in the nick of time. Before Jamie had managed to fuel this thing between them until it burned them both down.

Not daring to look back at her—afraid he would be haunted forever by what he saw in her eyes—Jamie brushed by her father and went out into the rage of the storm.

He felt empty and bereft.

CHAPTER ELEVEN

IT TOOK EVERYTHING Jessica had not to chase after Jamie. She turned to her father and he shoved his hands in his pockets.

"Dad! Really?"

He had a mulish look on his face. "I wanted to know if he's the one who hurt you."

"No one hurt me."

"When you came back from New York—"

"That's none of your business! And you shouldn't have come barging in here!"

"I came to check on you. I might have accidentally set the lock on the store. When you didn't come home I was afraid I locked you in."

"I would have called you if I needed you."

"It's bad out there tonight," her father said stubbornly.

"For Pete's sake, he wasn't my date for high school prom! I don't have a curfew! I'm an adult. You know what the problem is with Timber Falls? I can't grow up here. I can't grow at all!"

The words had come out in a rush of feeling. She saw she had hurt her father, and she was instantly sorry, even if it was so true that a complete stranger that she had met only for a few moments had seen it. Vivian Ascot had seen it before she had seen it herself. Jessica was trapped in a cozy, lovely life. If she wanted to be alive—fully and completely alive—she had to outgrow everything she had ever known.

She had to face her fear.

She left her father and went to find Jamie. She wanted to finish what they had started. Somehow it felt as if her life depended on it.

But when she got there, he had already left the B and B.

"I told him it wasn't a good night to go," Ethel Clariman said, worried, "but it seemed as if he couldn't get out of here fast enough. He left something for you, though."

Ethel went back into the office and came out with a large garment bag.

Jessica took it and got out of there as quickly as she could, hoping she had not looked as shaken as she felt that he was gone.

The hard truth was that he regretted what had

happened between them as intensely as she embraced it.

He couldn't get out of here fast enough.

She went home, opened the garment bag and slowly put on the blue dress. She twirled a few times in front of the mirror. This was the woman she could be. This was the woman she wanted to be. How much courage would it take to get there?

She went to bed in the dress. She let the tears come.

And the fear came out of the misty corners of her mind and showed itself to her.

She recognized the core belief that had ruled her entire adult life, had shaped every single decision, that had made her choose safety and security over boldness and full engagement.

In her mind, love equaled loss.

In her mind, the avoidance of pain had become paramount.

In her mind, love equaled the potential for the destruction of the entire world as she knew it.

It occurred to her it was not Jamie she had not trusted. It was herself. If the loss of Devon had crippled her for so long, what could the love of Jamie, so much hotter, so much brighter, do to her?

Leave her in ashes, obviously.

She had not trusted herself to be strong enough, and resilient enough to cope with what life and love gave her. To cope, to become more courageous, and more confident in her ability to survive.

So, each time life had given her a gift, she had turned away from it.

No thanks, that might hurt me.

Jamie had been a gift.

It was time to find what was at her core. It was time to rise to the challenges of life instead of shrinking away from them.

It was time to embrace love in all its capriciousness. In all its uncertainty.

In the morning, she picked up her phone and, with no hesitation whatsoever, she dialed his number.

It went straight to voice mail, which, given the complexity of the journey to Timber Falls, was not unexpected.

She listened to his voice. She listened to the beep. Jessica took a deep breath.

"I am not afraid to love you," she said, and then ended the call.

She slipped the phone into her pocket. She didn't feel as if she was waiting for a response. She felt as if she had set herself free.

For the first time in so, so long, she was not afraid.

Because she knew she was strong enough to handle whatever life gave her next. Three days passed, and she heard nothing. Still, her belief in what she had discovered did not flag. There was an ultimate gift in loving someone and in being open to love: it didn't rip you down, it didn't destroy you.

It made you better than you had ever dreamed you could be.

And then, after a week had gone by there was a tap on her cottage door.

She opened it and was stunned to find Jamie standing there. It wasn't until that moment when it started beating again that Jessica realized her heart had stopped when she had left him that message. Her heart had been waiting, even as she went on.

Jamie looked beyond haggard. He looked haunted. And uncharacteristically disheveled, his shirt wrinkled, his hair a mess that made her want to fix it with her fingers.

She was in her pajamas, she remembered suddenly, the ones with ducks on them. They did not make the statement about the new bolder, braver her that she wanted to make! She wanted to just close the door in his face, at least until she went and changed, but there was something there that was so tortured about him, that she could not.

Love told her this was not about her.

"Jamie?"

He looked as if he was going to reach out and touch her cheek, but then rethought it, and put his hand in his pocket. "I have a proposition for you," he said, his voice hoarse.

"Like a business proposition?" she said, and could not help but feel disappointment. It was just more of the same. Except it wasn't. Jamie would not be looking like he was looking for it to be just more of the same.

She thought of those lions at the library. One urged her to patience.

"Kind of like that."

"You should have emailed, then. It's a long trip." One that required fortitude.

"Can I come in?"

But she moved back from the door and he moved into her little space. It was so different from what he lived in, she wondered if he would laugh.

But he didn't. He looked around, and then back at her. He took in the pajamas and smiled. Even though his smile was tired, it lit the room and her heart. "It suits you."

She hoped he didn't mean the damned ducks on the pajamas.

"Not as much as it once did," she told him.

She gestured to a chair. It seemed too small for him. She took the couch facing him. Whatever his proposition was, she was saying no. Unless it was an indecent one, and then she would consider it.

"JHA wants you."

As she had suspected. Was he going to ignore the message she had left him?

"Vivian Ascot wants you."

Getting worse and worse.

"What about you?" she said, amazed at her own boldness.

"Well, therein lies the problem. I want you, too. Only I don't want you in the way they want you."

Her mouth went dry. "W-what?"

"I want you in a way that is completely inappropriate for a boss to want an employee. So we can't offer you a job, Jessica."

She realized she didn't care about the job.

"And of course I can't have you in the way I want you, either."

"Why not?" she stammered shamelessly.

"Ah, Jessica, we both know you aren't that kind of woman."

"I could be," she said.

"No, you couldn't. I realized that when your dad came in and found us. That you weren't that kind of woman and that you never would be. That you would compromise something integral to you if you tried to be."

"Maybe that's not for you to decide."

He sighed. "I felt sick with shame that night. I nearly did something I would have regretted forever. But I want a chance to try again. Only to do it right this time. To see if I can be the kind of man worthy of a woman like you."

"I'm afraid I don't understand."

"I want to be a man you never have to be afraid to love. Worthy of what you have held out to me.

I proposed to JHA and Vivian that we give you a private contract as a consultant. You can do everything you do best—run seminars and training sessions for bookstore owners—but you can still own your bookstore, too. You can go back and forth between New York and here. And I can go back and forth between New York and here. Because I've fallen in love with your world."

Her *world*, she told herself firmly. But then he went on.

"And I am falling for you. Unlike you, I'm afraid as hell of it. But I have a feeling you could teach me the meaning of courage, if I give you the chance."

It dawned on her, that's why he was here.

They were going to give this thing—this powerful, mysterious force that was blossoming between them—a chance.

"Because you don't work for me," Jamie continued softly, "and I won't be your boss, I can romance you the way a woman deserves to be romanced. Wooed, as the gals of the Smitten Word called it.

"I want to be that man, Jessica, the one who takes it slow and woos you and sees if what we have both been feeling over the last few days can go to where I want it to go. Where I hope you want it to go, too."

"And where is that?" she whispered.

"I'm hoping, one day, you'll be my wife. I'm hoping, soon, I'll be the guy so in love—so un-afraid of love—that I'll buy the most expensive engagement ring in the store window."

It was a pinch-me moment. She began to weep. And then to laugh. And then she wept some more. She had never felt joy as all-consuming as the joy of Jamie finding his way back to her, saying yes to all the possibilities love held out to them.

And then he was on the couch beside her, and he lifted her into his arms, and cradled her against the solidness of his chest and whispered love songs into her hair.

This was what she knew in that moment: this was the gift of having the courage to say yes to love. This place, her cottage, her parents, Timber Falls, none of these were home any longer. She did not need them, any longer, to feel the world was safe. And New York would not be home, either.

Home, that place of ultimate safety, where

you were accepted and celebrated for yourself, would be, from this day forward, wherever love led them.

EPILOGUE

I READ THE report in front of me with a good deal of pleasure. For a while it seemed as if my attempt to repay Jessica Winton her kindness to me that day in Copenhagen was going to backfire. I got a number of emails from her, snappy in tone, letting me know she was not happy with an old lady meddling in her life.

She even called me that. An old lady! Imagine.

"It's quite funny, isn't it?" I said to Max. "I thought she was going to be the easy one."

Max seemed quite bored with the discussion, and looked longingly at his cookie jar. The doctor has said I have to cut down on his cookies.

"Half," I told him, breaking one in two. He nearly took my hand off as he grabbed it and gulped it down. He acted as if he was starving, as if he had been doing doggie obstacle courses, instead of lying on my lap all day.

I hadn't planned the romance part of it. Of course, I wouldn't plan that. A romance is always a complication that, in my experience, life does not need.

And a romance with that man, the hyphenated name one. Even though I consider myself jaundiced about the topic, the thought of those two together—Jessica and Jamie, as I found out his first name is—pleases me in some way. Some people, maybe even most people, given time, seem to bring out the worst in each other, but somehow I believe those two will beat the odds.

I think they will bring out the best in each other.

"I'm getting soft in my old age," I told Max. I could see from his hopeful expression he thought that meant the other half of the cookie.

I felt a sudden and completely unexpected longing for the life I had not chosen. Family, that most complicated of things, and children.

I shook off the thought.

Family, to me, has always been a source of great pain, not an experience I was eager to repeat once I had escaped my own. The constant worry about the health and welfare of my doggie companions has shown me I didn't have the constitution to raise a child. The worry would have never stopped. If I'd had a child when I was twenty, that child would be in his or her fifties today, and I bet I would be as worried as the day they were born.

Maybe I would have had grandchildren, a forlorn voice inside me said wistfully.

No, I am better off alone. Me, with my gift for seeing so clearly what other people need, should have every confidence I have made the right choices about my own needs.

Still, I hope the other two young ladies are going to be easier, and not create such a sense of longing in me for the paths I had not taken.

Aubrey has been sick, poor thing. Not that there's any good person to get sick, but she's absolutely the wrong one: so independent and spunky. Her well-meaning brothers probably nearly suffocated her in their clumsy love. Well, hang in there, dear, all the adventures you ever longed for are coming at you soon.

And Daisy!

I've given Daisy the old house in Italy. She thought what she needed was success, as so many of us do, but I can tell you that it is not what it's cracked up to be. What she needs most is a place to call home.

Extravagant some people might say, but I don't see it that way.

With no family to leave all this to, why not be extravagant? I could walk down the street and give one-hundred-dollar bills to strangers for a whole week and not even make a dent in my fortune.

Maybe I'll do that. Next week. Me and Max.

But today, I feel ready for a nap. All this meddling, as Jessica so unkindly called it, has left me quite exhausted.

* * * * *

LET'S TALK
Romance

For exclusive extracts, competitions
and special offers, find us online:

📘 facebook.com/millsandboon

📷 @millsandboonuk

🐦 @millsandboon

Or get in touch on 0844 844 1351*

For all the latest titles coming soon,
visit millsandboon.co.uk/nextmonth

*Calls cost 7p per minute plus your phone company's price per
minute access charge

Want even more
ROMANCE?

Join our bookclub today!

5✓